THE DAY THE PARROT DIED

A Glendon Hills Retirement Center Mystery

Nancy Gotter Gates

Copyright 2012 by Nancy Gotter Gates

Published by Cottage Place Publishing

Book design by Karen Gates

First Edition

ISBN 13: 978-0985531300
ISBN 10: 0985531304

Library of Congress Control Number: 2012907983.

Acknowledgements

Thanks to the intrepid members of my writing group who always share their gift of critiquing that makes my work so much better: Harol Marshall, Lynette Hall Hampton, Betty DiMeo and Helen Goodman.

CHAPTER ONE

66Okay, Vi-OH-la, eat your Brussels sprouts. They're good for you."

That imperious command took me back seventy years to when I was five. My mother wouldn't let me have dessert till I'd eaten every bite of the detested vegetable. To make sure I paid attention when she wanted to make a point, she always emphasized the "O" in my name. A wanna-be musician, she'd named me after her chosen instrument, a relic handed down from her grandfather. The caterwauling sound she managed to elicit from it, which my father called the "Weatherspoon Wail," was the background "music" of my early childhood.

But my mother had died twenty-two years ago, and I was sitting in the dining room of the Glendon Hills Retirement Center. Its logo, a flowing intertwined G and H, is everywhere, woven into the carpet in the middle of the lobby, on the dinner plates and glassware as well as printed on every official piece of paper, so we fondly call it "Geezer Heaven" or simply GH. At least my best friend of eight months Ty Landowski and I do. Others might not appreciate our brand of humor. Ty and I were eating together as we do most nights.

"Listen, Ty-RONE, at my age I'll eat what I damn well please!" I gave him a stern look over the granny glasses perched on my nose. I like to see what I'm eating having once mistaken horseradish sauce for sour cream.

I knew he hated his first name as much as I hated mine. His mother had been enamored of Tyrone Power, a movie star wildly popular from the thirties to the fifties. Saddled with such unfortunate appellations, we prefer to be called Vi and Ty. But when we want to needle each other we resort to our formal names.

"So what are you up to this evening?" I asked him to direct his attention away from my food.

"The Bridge Dudes want to get a table or two together," he said.

The Dudes are a group of men who can't seem to get enough of the game. They play morning, noon and night if they can. I like to play occasional social bridge, but I am barely adequate at it. I'd be more than intimidated to play with any of them.

"How about you?"

"There's a good program on PBS tonight, a 'Live from Lincoln Center' production,'" I said. Frankly, I was just anxious to get out of my bra and into my jammies and robe. There ought to be a law that says once you reach seventy, you no longer have to wear the uncomfortable undergarments you've been forced to wear all your life. I happen to be a big, well-endowed woman to whom the word "dainty" has never been applied. I'm not fat, but I have a big frame, and I stand five-foot-ten inches tall, two inches taller than Ty. And bras have been a loathed item I've had to endure for well over sixty years.

For the record, I did *not* eat my Brussels sprouts, and I did have cherry pie with vanilla ice cream. Ty ate his sprouts because he happens to love them and passed on dessert. That's how he stays so slim. Most people who live here count their length of stay not by months or years but by pounds added. Try as one might, it's awfully hard not to partake of the food that someone else cooks for you. And, Brussels sprouts not withstanding, they serve good food here.

After dinner Ty and I said good night and I went off to my third-floor apartment while he headed toward the first floor lounge where two bridge tables are always set up.

My tortoiseshell cat, Sweetie, greeted me at the door ready as always to lead me into the adjacent kitchen. A rescued cat, she is constantly begging to be fed, as though perpetually afraid she's going to go hungry.

"I just fed you before I went to dinner. Don't tell me you've forgotten," I replied to her insistent meows. I admit to having my own "senior moments," but Sweetie is just two years old. One of the reasons I chose this retirement center was because they had the foresight to realize how important pets can be when you get old. Several I visited had a no-pet policy which meant I crossed them off my list immediately.

Against my better judgment I gave her a few treats. I'm not above giving bribes to keep the peace.

I'd just settled in front of the TV in my blue polka-dotted fleece robe when the phone rang.

"Auntie?" the voice said. It was my niece, Greta Holcomb, the reason I ended up here. I spent my entire career in upstate New York with various Girl Scout councils, the last twenty as an Executive Director. When I retired, I wanted to go some place that didn't normally have storms that dropped two feet of snow but not to Florida or California. I wasn't willing to give up the joys of spring and fall, my favorite seasons.

Greta lives here in Guilford City, North Carolina, halfway between the mountains and the beach, and as my only living relative since her mom, my sister, died, she urged me to move here. Actually she invited me to live with her and her husband, Cliff, though I had no intention of intruding into their lives. But I liked the idea of being near them, and Glendon Hills Center seemed to be the ideal choice. I could have bought a townhome or rented an apartment, but I thought being in a continuing care place would take the burden off of Greta should I become sick or disabled. Not that I expect that to happen anytime soon. I'm healthy as a horse and intend to stay that way for a long time to come, God willing.

"What's up, Greta?"

"I want to invite you and Ty for supper one night this week. Maybe we could play a few hands of bridge afterward."

Greta has been trying to promote something between Ty and me ever since she met him. At every opportunity she'll drop remarks about what a great guy he is and almost always includes him in invitations she extends to me. I get a real kick out of watching her trying to manipulate every situation to throw us together. The truth is neither of us is interested in a romantic involvement. Neither Ty nor I ever married, and we are both perfectly happy about it. Ty spent a lifetime working for the State Department in embassies all over the world. He's never said so, but I strongly suspect he worked for the CIA. We like and respect each other in spite of our needling and have a lot of interests in common, but that's all there is to it.

"I'd love to come to supper, but I'm not so sure about the bridge. You know what a mediocre player I am."

"Well, we could play Scrabble or something else if you'd rather."

"Let me ask Ty and I'll get back to you."

The next morning I went to my exercise class at eight. It's held in a large tiled-floor room on the bottom floor of our building where floor-to-ceiling windows overlook an expanse of lawn leading to the woods. It was late March, and the signs of spring were everywhere. The redbud trees on the lawn were in full fuchsia bloom, and in the woods the first pale white specks of blossoms on the dogwood trees promised they were nearly ready to burst forth. It was almost time for class to start, and Ty hadn't shown up. We usually meet in the little café which serves snacks and drinks and have a cup of coffee together fifteen minutes before the class starts, but he wasn't there at the usual time. I was getting a little anxious because he is always so punctual. Around here, if someone doesn't show when you expect them, you tend to think the worst. You are reminded almost daily of your mortality in a retirement home.

Just as Sarah Plunkett, AKA Spunky, strode to the front of the class, Ty rushed in the door and stood beside me. He's a slender, wiry guy with a full head of curly steel-gray hair that all the men secretly envy. They tease him about having hair transplants or wearing a "piece," but he finds the curls annoying and tries in vain to slick them down. He once threatened to shave his head, but I told him he'd look like a mafia don. What I didn't say was that his curls add a couple of inches to his height which isn't a bad thing.

"There was a slight panic on my wing," he whispered. "I'll tell you about it after class."

We had no time to talk as Spunky led us through our thirty minutes of aerobic exercises. Our fitness instructor is as vivacious as a cheerleader, and everyone loves her. She teaches many different levels of exercisc as well as pool exercise and yoga. No matter what a resident's disabilities are, there's a class for him or her even if it means working out in a chair. Luckily Ty and I are still able to keep up with the high level, but I know that as I age there will always be a class for me.

"You want to go to get some coffee now?" Ty asked as we exited the exercise room.

"Sure. I can always use another infusion of caffeine."

In the café, we each poured ourselves a cup from the dispenser on the counter and settled in at one of the tables. I loaded mine with a couple of shots of cream while Ty drank his black.

"So what made you late?" I asked.

"Ginger Willard came flying out of her apartment as I was on my way down here to meet you. She was hysterical."

"She tends to get hysterical over almost anything. Like the time she burned some toast, and the next thing she knew a bunch of firemen were storming through her door. I thought she was going to have a nervous breakdown over that incident."

Ty shook his head. "Yeah, those smoke detectors are so super sensitive I'm afraid to cook anything on top of the stove. One puff of smoke and the alarm goes off. But this time it was because she found her pet bird, Lester, dead in his cage."

I felt a stab of sorrow. As ditzy as Ginger was, I knew what it was like to lose a beloved pet, even a foul-talking parrot. The story I heard was her late husband Charlie peppered his conversations with colorful language, and the bird picked it up. Ginger probably loved Lester because he reminded her of her spouse. Frankly I found it embarrassing to visit with her and be constantly interrupted by Lester's expletives. But she blithely ignored him and acted as if nothing was amiss. Ginger herself was very lady-like and never used that kind of language. It made for a very surreal experience.

"So what did you do?" I asked.

"Well, she has no relatives nearby. So I called Babs and asked her to come up and be with her. She could help her decide how to dispose of Lester. I imagine she doesn't want him to go to the town dump."

Babs Osborn was the resident who had a background in counseling and seemed to know the right thing to do on almost every occasion. Everyone leaned on her when they had a problem.

"Great idea, Ty. Maybe they can arrange a little ceremony and bury him out in the woods."

"I thought we could stop by her apartment for a minute and give her our condolences. Are you game?"

"Sure." Secretly I wasn't eager to see Ginger knowing how distraught she could get. But I knew it would be the kind thing to do.

We walked together toward the East Wing. Our building has two wings that stretch out from the central lobby/dining room/café/office area. I live in the West Wing while Ty lives on the other side.

We took the elevator to the fourth floor where both Ty and Ginger live. The hall makes a Y with the elevator at the central point, and two wings go off at a 45-degree angle back to the left and right. We turned left to go down Ty's hall.

We'd barely turned the corner when we spotted someone halfway down the hallway standing motionless as a statue. As we drew closer, we realized it was Phyllis Duncan. Her beautiful white hair which was usually perfectly coiffed was in disarray, and her pale blue tee shirt was splattered with dark red spots. She stared straight ahead with a glassy stare. Most frightening of all, her right hand clutched a long, sharp kitchen knife held stiffly at her side. The lower half of the blade glistened with wet blood.

CHAPTER TWO

We both stopped in disbelief.

"Phyllis!" Ty barked.

She didn't respond. She seemed to be in another world.

"Phyllis!" he commanded again.

She didn't blink an eye.

I started to move toward her but Ty held out his arm in front of me to keep me in place.

"Stay back," he whispered. "I'll call security."

He carried his cell phone in a little holster on his belt. I always teased him asking if it was "loaded and ready," but now I was thankful he had it. He dialed the number and talked so softly I couldn't make out what he was saying.

"They'll be here in a minute or two," he whispered to me. "In the meantime I think it best I stay where I am and keep an eye on her. I don't think she's going to attack me. But I want you to back slowly down the hall and get out of here."

"No way," I said. "I'm not going. Two of us are better than one." What I didn't say was I probably had fifty pounds on him and could wrestle Phyllis to the floor if I had to.

"You are so stubborn, Vi-OH-la." He gave me a slight smile without taking his eyes off Phyllis.

The three of us remained in the standoff for the five minutes it took for someone to arrive. Brad, our daytime security man, dressed in dark trousers and white shirt with "Glendon Hills Retirement Center" embroidered over the pocket, and Ike, the biggest and burliest of our maintenance men in his dark blue work uniform and ball cap, strode purposefully toward us, beckoning Ty and me to retreat.

But we stood our ground as they came abreast.

"I think she's in shock," Brad said to us.

"We'll handle it," Ike said. "You two should go."

We backed up a few steps, but neither of us was willing to leave. Not only was our curiosity aroused, I was very concerned for Phyllis. I'm sure Ty was too. She was a relative newcomer to GH, a quiet little lady who kept very much to herself. Her husband, Ralph, on the other hand was outgoing and jumped into the life here with both feet. He'd been a salesman and seemed the prototype: a glad-hander and life-of-the-party who usually attended our social events without his wife. He tended to flirt with the ladies which didn't exactly win him any points with the husbands.

Phyllis chose to fix meals in their apartment rather than eat in the dining room which made her even more invisible. That struck me as odd. One of the best perks at GH was having someone else make your dinner. As far as I knew no one else did much cooking except to whip up a batch of cookies or a pot of soup now and then. But the Duncans never came downstairs for a meal.

When asked about Phyllis, Ralph's usual answer was that she "wasn't feeling well." She was something of a mystery to all of us. I'd called her a couple of times when she first moved in and asked if I could come over to introduce myself, but she always had an excuse: she was in the middle of an important task, she was about to take a nap, or some other reason, all of which struck me as half-truths at best. I finally gave up trying to be neighborly.

But what little I did see of her, she appeared very vulnerable. An aura of unhappiness clung to her like a cloak. Watching the two men approach her slowly, speaking to her in calming tones, I felt guilty for not having made more of an effort to get acquainted with her.

Brad finally got close to her and put out his hand, palm up, beseeching her to give him the knife.

She stared at him for a minute, and then slowly raised the weapon. I clutched Ty's arm as Ike bounded forward and grabbed her forearm giving it a twist. Her grip loosened and the bloody knife fell to the carpet. Then Phyllis crumpled to the floor.

While Brad knelt down and felt her pulse, Ike pulled his intercom off his belt and barked "Call 911. We need cops and an ambulance. Fourth floor east by apartment 423."

Ty and I ran forward to see if we could help.

"Did you see that?" Ike asked, stashing his intercom back in his belt. "She tried to stab Brad." He was visibly shaken. He took off his cap and ran his hand over his black curly hair before readjusting his hat squarely on his head, a gesture he frequently made when upset.

Brad, who was still holding her wrist said, "I don't think so, Ike. I think she was just trying to hand it to me."

"That lady was out of it. She didn't know what she was doing She was crazy, man."

Brad shrugged.

I was wearing a lightweight sweater because the exercise room tends to be chilly. I took it off and handed it to him.

"Why don't you roll this up and put it under her head?" I suggested.

Instead he spread it over her torso. "I think she's in shock. It's better to keep her warm. I hope you don't mind." I knew he was referring to the blood on her tee which looked so recent it could stain my sweater.

"No problem," I said. I knelt on the floor beside her and took her left hand in mine. It was ice cold. "I should have remembered that," I continued. "I was involved in enough disaster exercises when I was with the Girl Scouts. But the real thing is a whole lot different than seeing people smeared with ketchup. You don't always remember your training." I mentally excused myself on the basis we only did it once a year, not enough to make one truly proficient.

Ty stooped down beside me. "You know, guys, the burning question is where did the blood on the knife come from?" It was a question we all seemed to be avoiding.

"I'm going to check out the apartment to see if someone needs help. But I don't have a good feeling about this. If a crime has been committed, I'll let the cops handle it. I'm not going to be the one to mess up the crime scene," Brad said. "That's way beyond my duties."

He opened the door and entered, letting it close behind him. He was back in five minutes with a strained look on his face. "It looks like Mr. Duncan is dead. I checked his vitals but there was nothing I could do for him."

Several residents, having heard the commotion, came out of their apartments and were staring at the group of us huddled around the still figure of Phyllis. Since the knife was now beneath her and my sweater covered the stains on her tee shirt, they probably thought she had simply tripped or fainted. I wanted to keep it that way.

"We've called for help," I stood up and spoke to them. "Why don't you all go back in your apartments and let the EMTs take care of her. You don't want to get in their way."

Looking universally sheepish they retired to their respective apartments. There is always a lot of curiosity when one of the residents gets sick or hurt. Everyone wants to know what happened, but because of the HIPAA restrictions, the staff isn't allowed to pass on any information. So the rumor mill always gears up and news spreads quickly but not necessarily with accuracy. Inquisitiveness is always alive and well, but genuine concern plays a large role too. The people here honestly care deeply about each other.

It wasn't long before the EMTs arrived with a gurney along with a couple of Guilford City's finest. Brad explained the situation to the police while the medics checked out Phyllis. She was beginning to regain consciousness and tried to rise, but they insisted she remain lying down. When they finished checking her pulse and blood pressure, they removed my sweater and checked to see if she had any injuries that had caused the blood on her clothes. Satisfied there were none, they lifted her onto the gurney, preparing to take her to the ambulance.

One of the cops put up a hand to halt them.

"Just a minute, fellows. Let me speak to her for a minute."

The EMTs stood aside.

"What is her name?" the younger of the two police officers asked me.

"Phyllis Duncan," I said.

He went to her side and looked at her kindly. "Ms. Duncan, can you tell me what happened?"

She looked at him blankly and shook her head.

He tried again. "Don't you remember anything about the knife? Did you hurt someone?"

Her face reflected horror, but still she said nothing.

He waited a couple of minutes, but she closed her eyes and shook her head back and forth once more.

"Okay," he said to the medics. "Which hospital are you taking her to? Officer Jamieson will meet you there."

"Piedmont Emergency room," one of them said, and they continued to roll the gurney toward the elevator. The designated officer followed them down the hall. As they left, I realized that the knife still lay on the beige and green carpet staining it with blood. I had picked up my sweater and put it over my arm, folding the stained parts to the inside so they weren't visible.

"What about that?" I asked pointing at it.

"Evidence," the remaining officer said. "Don't touch it."

I wondered what they were going to do about it as residents began to come out of their apartments to go to various activities. It would be a little hard to explain away. I could just imagine what the rumor mill would say about that.

"There will be a lot of people in this hall shortly," Ty said. "My apartment is right there, 435. I've got a large waste basket. How about I invert it over the knife to protect it and also keep it out of sight?"

The officer stroked his mustache for a minute. "I guess that'll work. As long as you don't move it or touch it."

Ty went off to his apartment.

"Okay now," the remaining officer said. "Which apartment is hers?"

"Four-twenty-three," I said pointing to her door a few feet down the hall.

"You come with me," he pointed at Brad. "The rest of you stay here."

I was hoping Ty would get back with the wastebasket before the exodus began. Buses would take those residents shopping who no longer drove while others would be going to classes or pool exercises. In the meantime, Ike and I stood on either side of the knife hoping we could partially shield it if necessary.

"This is crazy," Ike lamented. "We never had nothing like this happen before."

"Like what?" I asked. "We don't know what happened. Ralph might have died of a heart attack. She could have been cutting up a beef roast and got excited or confused and ran out into the hall."

He rolled his eyes. "Some of the people here get mixed up sometimes, but they never did nothing like this. I don't think it was no beef roast."

I had no answer for him. Nothing is predictable at GH where the majority of residents have health problems of some sort including a few with the beginnings of dementia. Though the Memory Unit is available for them, those with spouses are often cared for in their independent living apartments. Some are inclined to wander, but usually their spouse or health care worker makes sure they are safe. None has ever caused any trouble. Though I barely knew Phyllis, I didn't have the impression that dementia was her problem. Depression was more likely.

Ty came hurrying out of his apartment carrying a very large wastepaper basket and he quickly inverted it over the knife and sat down on top of it.

"Good heavens," I said. "That's the biggest wastebasket I ever saw."

"Keeps me from having to go to the trash room as often," he said.

Just then Buck and Gladys Barlow came out of the apartment at the end of the corridor.

"What's going on?" Buck asked as he approached us.

I'd decided at the start to make up some kind of a cover story until we could get things straightened out.

"Someone had a little accident on the carpet," I said coyly. "We didn't want anyone to step in it till it could be cleaned up." Let them decide what the "accident" might be.

Ty was facing toward me, away from the couple, and he winked and gave me a sly grin.

Gladys grimaced, and Buck said, "That's good of you," as they carefully walked around us.

Other residents began emerging and I gave them the same story. They all seemed glad that we had hidden any unpleasantness. A few had seen Phyllis lying on the floor and asked about her. I told them she'd been taken to the hospital for observation, but I thought she'd be okay.

The exodus was complete by the time the cop and Brad emerged from the Duncan's apartment. Both looked quite grim.

"I've called CID," the cop said. "There's been an apparent homicide."

Although all of us, I'm sure, knew that something bad had happened in that apartment, I naively had hoped he'd died of natural causes. Of course that wouldn't explain the bloody knife, but I didn't want to believe the worst. That's why I'd made the dumb statement about a pot roast.

"Ralph?" I asked. I felt my face redden. I already knew he was dead. And unless they were hiding someone in their apartment, who else would have been murdered?

Brad frowned and nodded.

"Oh, my god," Ty and I said in unison.

The cop pointed to the wastebasket. "Is the knife under there?"

"Yeah," Ty answered. "No one's touched it."

"Why don't you folks move along then. We have things under control, and CID should be here shortly."

As curious as I was, I was reluctant to leave, but I didn't think I had much choice. I didn't want to go to downstairs where everyone would be pestering us with questions.

"Ty, why don't we go over to the hospital and see how Phyllis is doing?" I asked.

"She'll be under guard," the patrolman said. "They won't let you see her."

I felt totally frustrated and helpless. It seemed there wasn't a thing I could do.

"Okay, then. Ty, why don't we go out to lunch? I'd just as soon stay away from the dining room and inquiring minds."

Ty got up from the wastebasket. "Good plan, Vi. Let's do that."

CHAPTER THREE

I went back to my apartment to get a lightweight jacket and told Ty I'd meet him by the front door. Although I'm an excellent driver, Ty always wants to drive when we go places together. A man's prerogative I guess. But in his case I think it is because he has a love affair with his car.

The first thing I did when I got back to my place was to find a used grocery bag and place the sweater I was carrying in it. I probably could have gotten the stains out with some effort, but I couldn't imagine wearing it again knowing Ralph's blood had been on it. I took the bag to the nearest trash room and threw it in the dumpster.

I then grabbed a light jacket out of the front hall closet, gave Sweetie a few treats so she wouldn't follow me out into the hall, and left.

Ty was waiting in the outer lobby on one of the benches, away from any curious residents.

I joined him and we headed for the parking lot. The day was a little nippy but as beautiful as it had promised from our view in the exercise class. We climbed into his bright red little two-seater sports convertible. It's a comfortable fit for Ty but a bit of a squeeze for me. He loves the little car dearly and drives with the top down in all but the coldest or most inclement weather.

"Where to?" he asked.

I thought for a minute. "It's a little early to eat. How about a short ride out of town to enjoy the redbud before we go to lunch. Then I'm in the mood for some down-home food. How about Sammy's?" Sammy's was a little hole-in-the-wall family-run restaurant on Field Street.

"Sounds good," he said and roared out of the lot. Ty is a safe driver but he does push the speed limit a bit. I was glad I'd suggested the ride. It gave us a chance to decompress after the shocking events we had just witnessed. We'd never had anything remotely like it occur before, and it was so unexpected considering the perceived "safe haven" we'd always considered GH to be.

At Sammy's we both ordered their meat loaf special with mashed potatoes and gravy and black-eyed peas.

Once the waiter was gone I said, "What do you suppose is going to happen to Phyllis now?"

Ty shook his head. "Depending on what they find in the hospital, I'd guess they'd take her into custody if they don't have to admit her. On the face of it I'd say the evidence is quite damning."

"Oh, lord. She seems so frail mentally and physically. I don't know how she would survive it. Do you know if she has any family?"

"I've never heard of any. I think I heard Ralph say they were childless."

"Are they from around here? Do they have any friends or former neighbors who could give her support?"

"They came from Chapel Hill. Not sure why they didn't go into a retirement home there."

"Well, I don't think she's made friends at GH. I've never decided whether she's just shy or there's something more to it than that."

"Like what?" Ty asked.

"I'd only say this to you," I answered," because I have nothing concrete to base it on. But I've wondered if there was some abuse."

"Oh," Ty said. "I never thought of that. Maybe women are more in tune with such things."

"In any event, it looks as if Phyllis is very much alone in the world right now. I think someone—meaning us—needs to help her."

Ty smiled. "Ms. Altruistic. And just how can we do that?"

"Well, first of all I'm going to ask my niece's husband Cliff if he could get involved."

Ty looked puzzled for a minute. "Oh, yeah, he's an attorney isn't he?"

"A defense attorney as a matter of fact."

"Okay. Sounds like a plan. What if she doesn't have any money? What if she wants someone else?"

"I know he does some pro bono work. And if she's living at GH she must have some money, though perhaps not a lot. Maybe she wouldn't want him to help her. But I think it's worth talking to him anyway. Get his input."

"Are you going to wait and see what happens to her, or are you going to talk to him right away?"

"It just so happens my niece Greta asked me to bring you to dinner one night. So how about I tell her we want to come? It seems almost preordained, doesn't it?"

He smiled again and pointed his finger at me. "There'll always be a bit of the Girl Scout in you, won't there? You can't resist helping people."

"Isn't that why the good Lord put us here on earth? Life's tough enough, and we need to help each other out. Especially when we get old."

"You might think you're old, Vi, but you're sure young in spirit."

It was my turn to smile. "The secret is I feel about sixteen until I look in the mirror. Then I think 'Who is that wrinkly old gal anyway?' It's always a shock to realize it's me."

The waiter brought our meals, and we ate for a while in silence.

Finally Ty said, "You know we never did get to see Ginger. I wonder how she's doing."

"I'd forgotten about her. But then the death of a bird doesn't exactly compare to the death of a spouse."

"Of course you're right. But some people take the loss of a pet very hard. Maybe we ought to at least check on her."

I nodded. "I'll try to be compassionate. It's just that the bird was such a nuisance. It was very hard to carry on a conversation with its constant foul-mouthed squawks."

Ty laughed. "You gotta wonder what her husband was like. Evidently she loved him a lot though or she wouldn't have cared so much about Lester."

"Okay, now that we've decided to visit Ginger and talk to Cliff about Phyllis, what are we going to say to the other residents about what happened this morning? I don't want to be the one to spread the news." I didn't want to be the one to start any gossip. Especially when our knowledge of what happened was so sketchy.

"Let's just try to avoid everyone until the word gets out," Ty suggested.

"You mean we should sneak back into our apartments and keep a low profile for the rest of the day. We can wait till tomorrow to visit Ginger. I'm sure everyone will know about Phyllis by then."

"Sure. Why not? I don't think anything special is scheduled for this afternoon. And I don't know about you, but I'm stuffed from this lunch. I don't need anything but a snack tonight."

I agreed. That seemed the best plan of action for now.

We managed to creep back into the building without running into anyone. At least I didn't see a soul on the way to the west wing. The dining room had emptied and nothing much was going on at one-forty-five in the afternoon.

I spent the rest of the day paying bills and reading one of Margaret Maron's latest mysteries. I especially enjoy them because they are set in North Carolina and give me insight into my adopted state.

After an evening meal of toasted cheese sandwich and tomato soup I called Greta.

"Hey, Auntie," she said, having identified me through Caller ID. I still can't get used to people knowing it's me before I even open my mouth.

"Ty and I would love to have dinner with you," I said. I'd decided not to bring up the topic of Phyllis until we were all together. And maybe in a day or two I'd know a little more about her situation.

"How about tomorrow night around six?" she asked. It would be Wednesday and the sooner we could talk to Cliff the better so he could get involved right away. I was afraid she wouldn't want us to come until the weekend.

"Perfect. Can I bring anything?"

"Just yourselves. We're looking forward to seeing you."

And working on pushing us into a romantic relationship. Lots of luck, girl. It isn't gonna happen.

CHAPTER FOUR

The next morning I met Ty in the café before exercise class. We generally go on Monday, Wednesday and Friday, but we'd gone to the Tuesday class yesterday to make up for one we'd missed on Monday. I'd had a doctor's appointment, and he had to get his car checked out.

"Have you heard any rumors yet?" I asked.

"Not yet," he said. "But the cat's out of the bag. There's crime scene tape across the Duncan's door. The *Gazette* had a small article on an inside page, but it only indicated that Ralph died under 'unexplained circumstances' without giving details."

I get the Guilford City *Gazette* as well, but I'd overslept and had to hustle to get to the café at our usual meeting time. When I didn't see anything about the Duncans on the front page, I didn't look any further.

"How strange is that? Do you suppose the powers-that-be here are trying to keep a lid on it as long as possible? You can imagine how this is going to affect their image and sales."

"I'm not sure they have that kind of clout," Ty said. "The cops are probably trying to sort things out before giving any details."

"Have you heard what people around here are saying?" I asked.

."I didn't see anyone on my way here. But I'll bet exercise class will be buzzing."

"Why don't we go down a little early and see what we can learn."

When we walked into the exercise room there was a huddle of people gathered around Cora Lee Hellman. Cora Lee always seems to know the latest about everyone, whether it's true or not.

We walked up close to hear what was being said.

Gladys Barlow noticed us. "Ty! And Vi!" she exclaimed. "You guys were there when the EMTs came to get Phyllis. Now the paper says Ralph died. What's going on?"

"You know as much as we do," I said. "I think she was distraught and fainted in the hall."

"Right," said Ty, backing me up. "I think it was such a shock to her system she passed out."

"But why the crime scene tape?" Cora Lee demanded. "That certainly isn't the norm when somebody dies around here."

I just shrugged my shoulders and tried to look bewildered. I couldn't think how to explain that away. But they weren't getting any more from me.

Spunky came in then and started the exercise class which got us off the hook.

After class we went to see Ginger, a visit I wasn't looking forward to. She was still in her robe looking pale and drawn when we knocked on her door.

"Hello, Ginger," Ty said in his most consoling voice. "We heard about Lester and came to tell you how sorry we are."

All I could do was nod in agreement. My heart wasn't in it though.

She opened the door wide. "Come in," she said in a melancholy voice.

The apartment was furnished with antiques or pseudo-antiques. I have no eye to judge whether they are the real thing or just copies. In the corner by the big picture window was a large empty cage on a pedestal with a huge black bow perched on the top.

Ty and I seated ourselves on the Victorian sofa covered in a moss green fabric. Ginger sat across from us in a rosewood chair with a carved back and needlepoint seat.

Ty and I sat for a minute trying to come up with something comforting to say. Finally I asked, "And how old was Lester?" After I said it I think I blushed. What kind of a dumb question was that? But I was feeling desperate for the appropriate words.

That brought on tears. "He was twenty-three," she said, wiping the tears away with the sleeve of her robe.

"That sounds like a ripe old age," Ty said trying to put the best face on it.

"Oh, no," cried Ginger. "He was an African Gray, and they can easily live to be fifty years old or more. He'd been just fine when I went to bed the night before, but in the morning I found him dead on the bottom of his cage. I can't imagine what happened to him."

I could tell Ty was as flummoxed as I was. We were trying so hard to give solace, but we seemed to be making matters worse.

Finally I asked, "Did Babs come and see you yesterday? She's always so helpful when tragedies happen."

I almost choked on the word "tragedy" when a real one had happened just down the hall, but I'm sure she considered it to be one.

"Yes she did. And she and I found a lovely box to put Lester in. It was a metal one meant for keeping files or important papers, but we lined it with silk that I had in my sewing basket and it made a nice little casket. We took it out there to the edge of the woods and buried him." She pointed out the window as she wiped a tear from the corner of her eye. "I found a large rock to mark the grave. Babs was so sweet to help me."

"She's very kind hearted," I said and thought *and pretty nonjudgmental too. She has a lot more patience than I would.*

We all sat in silence for a minute or two. I was trying to think how I could gracefully escape without seeming rude.

"Did something happen on our hall yesterday?" Ginger finally spoke. "When we got back from the little service we had for Lester, we saw people coming in and out of the Duncan's place who looked like officials of some kind. But I haven't left the apartment since then, so I don't know what's going on around here."

Ty looked at me and I looked at him, wondering how much to say. Finally I spoke up. "It said in the paper this morning that Ralph Duncan died. And apparently Phyllis went into shock or something. They had to take her to the hospital."

Ginger's hand went to her mouth. "Oh my gosh. Two deaths on the same hall in one day! That's awful!"

It seemed offensive to me to equate Ralph's death with that of her parrot, but I kept my mouth shut.

Ty looked at his watch and frowned. "Ginger, we've got to run. We've got some errands to do. But we just wanted you to know how sorry we were."

She sniffled. "Thank you. You're so kind."

She got up with us and saw us to the door. Once the door closed behind us I made a gesture of wiping my brow, and Ty shook his head and smirked. "Takes all kinds," he said in a whisper.

Ty had an afternoon bridge game planned, and I needed to do some grocery shopping. We decided to meet at my apartment at 5 pm to listen to the local news before going to Greta's. Sweetie greeted me at the door as always when I went home to get a sandwich before going to the store. I looked at her precious little face and felt ashamed of myself for feeling so condescending toward Ginger. I knew I would feel pretty damn bad if anything happened to my cat.

Ty was there a little before five which was a good thing because the story was the first on the news broadcast.

"The Guilford City police have charged Phyllis Duncan, 72, with the murder of her husband Ralph, 76. The incident took place yesterday in their apartment at the Glendon Hills Retirement Center on Revolution Road. Mrs. Duncan is currently under observation at Piedmont Hospital, but will be scheduled for arraignment as soon as she is released by the doctors. The Duncans recently moved here from Chapel Hill. There are no further details at this time."

"I guess the cat's out of the bag now," I said. "Poor Glendon Hills. This isn't going to help their reputation or sales." Marketing was having trouble trying to fill up the place under normal circumstances. When the housing market went belly up, many seniors who were planning to move to retirement homes had to scrap their plans knowing they could not sell their houses, at least not for anything near the price they had expected. And with the simple fact that the turnover here is high due to residents moving to assisted living or nursing care or simply passing away, it was like musical chairs. People are constantly moving in and out. With this incident happening, it was going to be tougher than ever to keep the place filled.

"Whatever happened?" Ty wondered aloud. "Do you think she suddenly went berserk?"

"That sounds like a possible defense. That or being the victim of abuse."

"Really? I know you mentioned that before. Do you have any reason to suspect he abused her?"

"Nothing concrete," I said. "But she always seems so withdrawn. She never participates in anything. Yet Ralph was the original glad-hander. Always thumping everyone on the back. Acting like the super-extroverted salesman even when he had nothing to sell. Not only that, he tended to hit on some of the women. I don't know why, but that always made me suspicious." *I didn't add that I wasn't among the women he hit on. Possibly he thought I was too intimidating, or maybe he didn't find me interesting.*

"That's kind of a flimsy argument," Ty said.

"I know. I do tend to jump to conclusions. Well, enough of that. We've got to get to my niece's house."

Greta greeted us at her door. She and Cliff live in an upscale neighborhood in Guilford City about a mile from Glendon Hills.

Nathan Park is arguably the classiest neighborhood in the city. Laid out in the 1920s by a nationally known architect, its imposing homes surround a beautiful country club and golf course. The Holcomb's house looks out over the seventh hole with its bright emerald putting green and undulating fairway. It's at its most beautiful this time of year because the golf course is filled with redbud and dogwood trees as is their backyard. The house is an English Tudor which they remodeled to include an up-to-the-minute kitchen and bathrooms that blend with the style of the home. The rear of the house consists mainly of huge windows or French doors that look out on their gorgeous backyard that merges onto the fairway. If I were young and had unlimited resources, it was exactly the kind of house that I would love to have. Except of course I have never needed four thousand square feet or more of space to live in alone. It might be my dream house, but in reality it would be entirely out of the realm of possibility both practically and financially. My eight hundred square feet at GH is perfectly adequate.

"Hi guys," Greta said giving each of us a hug. "Come on in."

She took our jackets and led us into the huge living room where a fire was lit in the gorgeous fireplace. The evenings get a bit nippy once the sun goes down this time of year.

Greta looks so much like my late sister, Wanda, it's almost scary. Since Wanda and I had a lot of similar features, Greta has been mistaken more than once for my daughter. We both have round faces, ski-slope noses, and rather startling green eyes. Our hair used to be the same auburn color until mine turned gray some years ago. I never could be bothered to keep it colored. While I keep mine cut very short for convenience, Greta wears hers in a page boy. She has the same stocky build as I do but she works out constantly in an effort to be as slim as possible. Ty once referred to her as "Little Vi," not only for our resemblance, I'm sure, but for the fact her figure is considerably smaller than mine. I chose to ignore him. And I'm not so sure she considers it a compliment.

Cliff rose from the sofa where he was sitting to greet us. Cliff is a handsome man, tall and slender with thick dark hair that may or may not owe its color to Grecian Formula. His square face and rather aquiline nose defy the theory that people are attracted by those with similar features. He is very much at ease with people which makes him, I would guess, quite effective in the courtroom.

"Hello, hello," he greeted us enthusiastically. "So good to see you two. We always pleased when you can join us for dinner." I'm sure that Greta has put a bug in his ear about promoting a romantic relationship between us.

We settled onto a facing sofa while Cliff went to fix us before-dinner drinks. It gave me a minute to admire, once again, the beautiful room. Greta is an interior designer, and the room nicely reflects her abilities. I don't know much about design, but I know what I like. The room is neither traditional nor modern, but an interesting mix. New furniture like the facing sofas with simple lines covered in teal contrast with old pieces like the scarred wooden box that possibly once held tools which serves as a coffee table between them. The whole room is an eclectic mix of wonderful objects gathered from all over as the Holcombs are avid travelers.

Cliff brought our drinks, white wine for me and Greta, and a whiskey sour for Ty. Cliff always has a Vodka Martini.

"So how are things at Glendon Hills?" he asked after sitting back down.

I'd planned to wait until later in the evening to bring up Phyllis, but this was the perfect opening.

"Well," I said, "glad you asked. Truth is we've had quite a tragedy there."

Greta sat forward in her seat, eyes wide. "Really! What happened?"

"One of our residents is being charged with killing her husband."

I could see Cliff's look of wariness. I'm pretty sure he knew where I was going with this. He said nothing as Greta asked the questions. Greta loved gossip as much as anyone at GH.

"Go on," she said. "Tell us more."

So I told her how we ran into Phyllis in the hallway with the knife in her hand. I described how Brad, our security man, made her drop the knife and she fainted on top of it.

"When the emergency guys took her away the bloody knife was lying in the middle of the hall. Ty, here, was quick thinking. He got a big wastebasket and covered it up. We didn't want the other residents to freak out."

"Bravo." Greta said. "But weren't the others curious why you had a wastebasket upside down in the middle of the hall?"

"I intimated that there was something nasty underneath," I said. "Of course there was, but I'm sure they thought it had something to do with bodily functions."

Greta made a face. "I guess that was quick thinking, Vi. But...yuck."

"You gotta do what you gotta do. Life can get pretty real in a retirement center."

Ty simply shrugged. "You don't want to start a panic in that place."

"So what happened then?" Greta asked.

Cliff was leisurely sipping his cocktail taking it all in.

"Brad and later the police went into the apartment. When they came out, they told us Ralph, her husband, was dead. We can only assume he was stabbed to death," I said.

Ty spoke up. "The five o'clock news tonight said they were charging her with murder and she would be arraigned as soon as she was released from the hospital."

For a couple of minutes no one said anything.

Finally I took the bull by the horns. "Cliff...?"

He stared at me for a minute and then a slow grin appeared. "Yes Vi?" I could tell he was going to give me a hard time and make me beg.

"This poor lady has no relatives around that we know of. She seems to be all alone in the world." I decided to play my ace. "I don't have any proof, but I suspect there might have been abuse."

"And why do you think that?"

"She's this mousy shrinking violet. Her husband was hail-fellow-well-met over-the-top sort and pretty obnoxious. We hardly ever saw her. But when we did, she seemed withdrawn and sorrowful. Something wasn't right."

"That's all you have to go on?"

I nodded. "That and my gut feeling."

Ty spoke up. "Vi has some pretty dead-on gut feelings."

Cliff laughed. "I can see where this is going. Why don't you just come out and say it, Vi?"

"Okay, Cliff, I will. Would you be willing to at least talk to this poor lady? Someone needs to help her out, and I'd hate to see her assigned some public defender. But, mainly I don't want her to have to spend any time in jail. Could you at least see that she gets out on bail?"

He sipped his cocktail some more while he thought about it.

"Oh, for heaven's sake, Cliff. Stop giving Vi a hard time. Tell her you'll do it," Greta demanded.

He slowly and deliberately set his cocktail glass on the coffee table. "For you, Vi, I'll do just about anything. Give me the name and particulars about this lady. I'll check it out tomorrow."

"Oh, thank you so much, Cliff. This means a lot to me."

"Now what do you say we go eat dinner?" Cliff said.

CHAPTER FIVE

I waited around the next morning on pins and needles waiting for Cliff to call. I usually go to the pool on Tuesdays and Thursdays, the days we don't have exercise class, but I was afraid I'd miss him. I participate in the Masters program for senior athletes in the swimming competitions. I specialize in breast stroke and have done fairly well in the state championships. I do it mostly to keep in shape and for the friends I've made at the meets. It's a wonderful program with something for everyone from pole vaulting to table tennis which is Ty's specialty. He has a fistful of ribbons to prove his skill. While I avoid playing bridge with him, I will on occasion play a game of ping pong knowing full well he'll beat the stuffing out of me.

Cliff finally called me around one in the afternoon.

"They're going to discharge Mrs. Duncan from the hospital shortly. I'm trying to schedule a quick arraignment hearing so she won't spend any time in lockup."

"Oh, I hope she doesn't have to. That would be devastating for her. But if she's charged with killing Ralph, will they even set bail?"

"She could be charged with anything from involuntary manslaughter to first degree murder. I doubt very much they will go for murder one. And her physical and mental health is so fragile right now it wouldn't be in the DA's best interest to keep her locked up. I'll let you know what happens ASAP."

Not long after I hung up from him Ty called. "Have you heard anything?"

"Phyllis is about to be released from the hospital, and Cliff is trying to get an arraignment hearing right away so he can post bond."

"Good. So if they bring her home, what are we going to do?"

"I'm not sure. I guess we should play it by ear. But I want to do whatever I can to help."

"The guys asked me to play bridge. I told them I might have to leave early so they have a backup ready. Come and get me when you hear she's coming home."

"Okay."

It was about four o'clock when Cliff called me on his cell phone "I'm on my way to Glendon Hills with Mrs. Duncan. I should be there in about fifteen minutes."

I hurried down to the lounge where two tables of bridge were in full swing. Ty was playing the hand and concentrating so hard on the cards he didn't even see me. When I tapped him on the shoulder, he jumped.

"Sorry," I said. "Finish your hand. But we've got something we need to do."

"Yeah, just a sec," he said. "I'm trying to make a little slam here."

I backed away so as not to make him nervous. I always marvel at how intense the guys can get over a little game.

Within five minutes Ty and his partner let out a victory yell. "Made it! Seven hundred rubber!"

Rubber, slam—how silly is that? I never understood where the terms came from.

Ty stood up. "Sorry fellas. Call Tom. He said he'd play for me if I had to leave."

He and I strode out into the hall. "So is she back in her apartment?" he asked.

"No. Cliff called and said he'd be here in a few minutes. I thought we could meet her at the front door and escort her home. Run interference if anyone tries to approach her."

"What? Are you thinking of keeping her isolated?"

"No, of course not. I just thought today she didn't need a lot of inquisitive people hanging around. We can take her up to her apartment and ask if she wants us to stay or not. If not, we'll tell her to call us whenever she needs us."

"Are you sure you weren't a counselor in another life?" Ty asked.

"Believe me, when you work for the Girl Scouts you learn to be all sorts of things including counselor, drill sergeant, salesman, and a whole lot more."

We were nearing the front door when I saw Cliff drive up in his big silver sedan. We hurried out to meet them.

Cliff got out of the driver's seat and went around to open the door for Phyllis. She'd always been small and frail looking, but now it seemed as if she'd shriveled up into a little wrinkly doll or maybe a puppet because she moved spastically as if someone else was controlling the strings to her arms and legs. He helped her out of the car and held her elbow as they proceeded up the walk.

We met them halfway to the door. I noticed Phyllis was wearing a blue scrubs top that hung on her frame. I never thought about her blood-spattered tee shirt. The cops had probably taken it for evidence. I should have gotten her a clean top somehow but it had never occurred to me.

"Hello, Phyllis," I said. "You might not remember me. I'm Viola Weatherspoon. And this is Ty Landowski your neighbor."

She squinted up at us. "I remember you," she said pointing at Ty. "You're the one who puts my newspaper in the door handle so it's easy for me to reach in the morning."

I didn't know he did that. But typical of him.

She looked at me. "I have a bad back so it's hard for me to bend over to get it off the floor. I think I remember you too. Do you live in the East Wing?"

"No, I'm in the West."

"Oh, I don't know many people over there. I don't get out much."

We were standing in the middle of the sidewalk chatting rather inanely, and I knew Cliff must be itching to get back to his office. He'd gone way out of his way to bring Phyllis home as it was. I didn't want to hold him up any longer.

"Mr. Holcomb needs to get back to work," I said. "Ty and I will take you back to your apartment."

All of a sudden she became rigid. "Oh, no. I don't want to go back there."

"But you must, Phyllis. Where else can you go? We'll stay with you for a while."

She grimaced. "No, no, I can't. There's blood all over the carpet."

Oh my god. I never thought of that. Of course there must be. What could we do?

I thought for a moment. "You can come home with me, Phyllis. I have a sofa bed in my den. Ty will go to management and get your carpet replaced as soon as possible. You can stay with me till it's done."

Ty took her hand. "I'll take care of it, Phyllis. Don't you worry. Just go on home with Vi."

She looked a little dubious but seemed to realize there was no other option. "Okay," she said. She turned to Cliff. "Mr. Holcomb, you have been wonderful. Thank you so much."

He smiled his most comforting smile. "Glad I could help. You have my card, Mrs. Duncan. Call me anytime. In the meantime I'll be working on your case."

The word "case" apparently resonated with her and her face crumpled. She seemed on the verge of tears.

I gently took her arm. "Let's go to my place, Phyllis. I'll make you comfortable, then if you'll give me your key, I can go get you some clothes and whatever else you'll need out of your apartment." Ty had told me the crime scene tape was no longer across her door.

She nodded, but she seemed almost in a stupor. I took her arm by the elbow and led her inside the building after thanking Cliff profusely.

He gave me a smile that bordered on a grimace and got back in his car and drove away.

"I'm on my way to see Frank," Ty said. Frank Kaufman was the Director of Operations at GH and handled all the physical parts of the building. If I knew Ty, he'd have the offending carpet gone by noon tomorrow.

I had to walk slowly with Phyllis. It was almost as if her limbs were disconnected from her brain. I think it was more emotional than physical. Everything was out of sync.

A couple of people started to approach us, but I signaled them away by shaking my head. She didn't need to encounter anyone in her frame of mind no matter how good their intentions.

It seemed to take forever, but we finally arrived at my apartment. I led her to my favorite chair, a large blue recliner, and told her I was going to fix up a bed for her in the den. She collapsed into it and seemed to almost disappear in its generous proportions. I got some sheets and a lightweight blanket out of the linen closet, pulled open the sofa bed and made it up. I had an extra pillow on my own bed that I never used and put on a clean pillow case. When I'd gone grocery shopping, I'd picked up an inexpensive bouquet of daisies and glads which I'd put in a simple glass vase on my dining table. I moved it to the table beside her bed.

I went back out into the living room. "Would you like to lie down for a while?" I asked.

She nodded her head yes.

"Before you do, it's not too long till dinnertime. Would you like me to bring our dinners up here tonight? I'm afraid I'm not much of a cook, and I don't have a lot of food on hand."

"I'm not hungry," she said.

"Well, you might be a little later. I'm going to order our dinners now. I've got the menu in my desk." Each Sunday we are given a weekly menu, and we can eat in the dining room or order it in advance and take it to our apartments. The food selection is generous so I don't know why I ordered Brussels sprouts earlier in the week. I guess I thought it was time I learned to like them but then realized it wasn't meant to be.

I read the selections from the menu to her, but she still insisted she didn't feel like eating. So I called the dining room hotline and ordered two identical meals hoping she'd regain her appetite.

Before I took her into the den I asked if I could have the key to her apartment and what clothes she might need from it.

"You'll have to get a pass key from downstairs," she said. "Mine's in my purse inside the apartment. And I don't know what I want. A nightie, some underwear, slacks and a top. Anything." It seemed almost too much of an effort for her to think about it.

I helped her onto the bed then quietly went downstairs to the front desk. Patricia is our receptionist, hand-holder, gate keeper to the administrative office, fountain of knowledge and everything in between. She doles out greetings, mail that doesn't fit in our boxes, and information. If anyone knows what goes on around here it's Patricia.

I explained to her about my need for a key to the Duncan's apartment.

"I saw you bringing her in, but she looked so lost I didn't even try to speak to her," she said. "How's she doing?"

"Not well at all," I said. "Ty is trying to get something done about the carpet in her place and in the meantime she's staying with me. So if you get any calls for her, send them my way."

"Sure will. And here's a key you can use. Be sure to bring it back when you find hers. And good luck. I think you're going to need it."

I grimaced. "Thanks." I wasn't looking forward at all to going into that apartment

CHAPTER SIX

I opened the door to Phyllis's apartment with trepidation, and my worst fears were realized. A large irregular circle of dried blood stained the white carpet in the middle of the living room. No wonder she didn't want to come back here. I was kind of surprised that management hadn't already done something about it, but they probably didn't have a chance since the police had taken down the crime scene tape so recently. I hoped Ty could expedite it.

I'd brought my large tote with the big bright sun with a smiley face that seemed woefully inappropriate right now. I went into the bedroom to find some clothes. The bed was still unmade as if the Duncans had just gotten out of it. I shivered. How life can be turned upside down in the fraction of a second.

I found a couple sets of underwear, a nightie, and socks in the dresser and two pairs of slacks and knit tops in the closet which I folded and placed in the tote. I was counting on the best-case scenario that Phyllis would be able to return home in a day or two.

While the rest of the house was extremely neat with the exception of the unmade bed, the bathroom was in disarray. A hair dryer was on the sink along with opened makeup bottles, toothpaste with the cap off and wet towels on the floor as if someone had been interrupted getting ready for the day. I picked up the makeup and deodorant and stowed it in my tote. Since there were two toothbrushes, I didn't know which one was hers, but I had a stash of extra ones I accumulated from trips to the dentist. I looked around and didn't see anything else that seemed necessary which I couldn't provide.

I wondered about medication. Most everyone my age is on some kind of pills. I decided to look in the kitchen which is where I keep mine since a lot of medicine should be taken with food. I had to pass through the living room again on my way there. When I looked at the stain, I couldn't believe how much blood the human body holds. I knew the scene would be in my nightmares for nights to come.

I was right about her pills. A plate on the kitchen counter held a number of pill bottles. I checked the labels before I put them in the tote. I didn't want to take any of Ralph's medicine along that could trigger another emotional crisis for Phyllis.

I found her purse in the hall closet and checked to make sure her house key was in it then added it to the tote as well.

I returned to my apartment and found that Phyllis was asleep so I quietly set the tote on the floor near her bed, and went back downstairs to return the key to Patricia. As I was standing at the desk, Ty came out of the administrative offices.

"Well?" I asked.

"They'll try to get it done tomorrow," he said. "Good thing it's Thursday or it would have had to wait till the first of the week."

"I don't mind at all having her stay with me," I said. "But she would probably be much happier in her own home, the sooner the better."

"What are you doing about supper?"

"I ordered ours to go. I'm just about ready to pick them up."

"Do you want me to join you?"

"She's asleep, Ty. She claims she isn't hungry. So I'll put hers in the fridge and try to talk her into eating it later when she wakes up. I'm going to eat mine and watch the news."

"Okay. Why don't I call you in the morning and see if you need anything. And I'll stay on top of this carpet thing and make sure it gets done."

I went back to the apartment and ate on a TV tray in front of the set. The lead story on the six o'clock news was about Phyllis. She had been charged with second degree murder, and the judge set bail at a million dollars. That meant a bail bond would cost a hundred thousand. How did I know this? Because I read a lot of mysteries. I wondered how Phyllis, or Cliff, came up with that amount of money. I was glad she was asleep, though I would not have turned on the news had she been awake and sitting in the living room with me.

Phyllis awoke around nine, though I think she would have preferred to sleep around the clock to avoid reality. She decided she was a little hungry so I popped her dinner into the microwave and heated up the chicken breast, broccoli, and mashed potatoes. She ate a few bites and claimed she was full. I was sure her capacity for food was limited as small as she was, but at that rate she was going to fade away to nothing. But I couldn't convince her to eat any more. I hoped her appetite would increase as the days went by.

As curious as I was about the events on Tuesday, I didn't think she was in any shape to talk about them that evening. So I tried some small talk but it mostly fell flat. She seemed unable to do anything but turn inward and brood about her situation. And I couldn't figure out how to steer her away from that. I switched on the TV to a nature channel and watched animals migrating on the Serengeti for a while, hoping it might catch her interest. But her thoughts were elsewhere, and she ignored it. Finally it was past my bedtime so I told her to make herself at home, but I was going to bed.

When I got up in the morning I found Phyllis, still fully dressed, sleeping soundly in my recliner with Sweetie asleep in her lap. I hoped the cat had given her some solace. I knew it always worked for me when I was down.

Ty called around nine, and the ringing of the phone woke Phyllis up.

"Anything I can do?" he asked.

"Not right now."

"Then I'm going to check to see if the carpet people are here. I want to keep on top of it."

When I hung up, Phyllis set Sweetie on the floor and struggled out of the chair.

"I guess I'm kind of hungry now," she said to me. Well, that was a good sign.

"I brought you some clothes. Why don't you go shower and change while I fix you some breakfast."

I had some frozen waffles and scrambled some eggs. I'd made a big pot of coffee for my own breakfast and there was plenty left. I set a place at my two-seat table in the kitchen and tried to fancy it up a little with a place mat, which I never use for myself, and a linen napkin (I always use paper). I brought the bouquet from the den and put it in the middle of the table.

Again she ate only a few bites before she pushed the plate away, but I figured something was better than nothing.

"Do you know when I can get back into my apartment?" Phyllis asked.

"They're supposed to replace the carpet today. Ty's checking on it and will let us know when it's done."

She began to cry. "I just want to go home," she wailed.

I got up from my seat at the table and put my arm around her shoulders. "I know you do, honey. We'll get you there as soon as we can."

I cleared up while she went back to the living room. I'd hidden the morning paper because I didn't want her to read about herself.

When I joined her, she seemed to be back in her funk again, slumped in the recliner. I noticed she'd picked up Sweetie again and was petting her with quick nervous strokes.

I was trying to make some non-threatening conversation to fill the void when suddenly she burst out, "I didn't do it! I didn't kill my husband!"

"Do you feel like talking about it?" I asked. I was nervous about pushing it for fear of sending her over the edge. I was afraid she could be on the verge of a nervous breakdown.

But she suddenly seemed to have an urgent need to tell me all about the events of that day.

"We'd slept late that morning because we'd stayed up the night before to watch a movie. It was a little before eight when I woke up. Ralph was still asleep so I decided I'd take a shower and get dressed before I fixed breakfast. I was in the bathroom for a while because I washed my hair and had to dry it. But before I was done, I heard a loud thump. I was afraid Ralph had fallen. So I ran out and found him lying in the middle of the living room covered in blood. There was this big kitchen knife on the floor beside him. I was so scared, Vi! I didn't know if someone was still hiding in our apartment and was going to jump out and stab me too or what. So I picked up the knife to defend myself and ran out the door. I don't know what happened then. It was like I went into shock or something. I couldn't seem to move or talk or anything. That's the last thing I remember till I woke up in the hospital."

"Did you tell the police that story?"

"Of course I did!" She was incensed. "They asked me if I had locked the door the night before. I told them I had. And Ralph always doubled checked it after I went to bed. He was such a stickler about safety."

"Was it unlocked when you ran into the hall?"

She looked startled for a moment as if she hadn't thought about it before. "No. I remember now. I had to throw the deadbolt. Oh my god. How could that be?"

"But you think someone came in and killed Ralph."

She threw up her hands. "Of course! There's no other answer. They must have locked the door when they left."

"And the cops don't believe you?" Poor naïve soul. She probably never realized what a hole she was digging for herself when she told them about the door being locked. A more sophisticated person would realize the ramifications and lie about it. I wonder if they'd Mirandized her or decided they weren't "holding her as a suspect" so they could use anything she said.

Her eyes teared up and I was afraid she was going to fall back into her zoned out state. But she rallied.

"They said there was no way anyone could get into my apartment without a key. And only management and the women who clean the apartments have pass keys. They questioned all the staff and were certain none of them were near my apartment at the time. Everyone could account for their whereabouts. They talked to the residents where the housekeepers were working and they all vouched for them."

I thought for a minute. "Yeah, the housekeepers are on the West Wing on Tuesdays. They don't do the East Wing until Thursday and Friday." I had to admit that having weekly housekeeping services was one of the best perks at GH. It was the first time in my life I hadn't had to scrub my own floors, clean the bathroom or change the bed.

Phyllis began to cry. "What am I going to do, Vi? What am I going to do?"

I leaned over toward her and took her hand. "Cliff's a very good lawyer. He'll do everything in his power to see that this gets straightened out."

"But it seems like everything is stacked against me. I don't know what he can do."

"Just leave it in his hands. I'm sure everything will work out."

I'm good at platitudes, but in my gut I wasn't so sure that was true. To the best of my knowledge Cliff was a caring and conscientious lawyer. But he was up against some daunting odds.

CHAPTER SEVEN

M y doorbell rang, and I went to open the door. It was Ty.

"Come on in," I said, scowling and nodding my head toward the living room to warn him things were not going well.

He silently confirmed he got the message.

"Phyllis and I were just chatting," I said. "Can I get you a cup of coffee?"

"No thanks," he said as he followed me. "I just had a quick cup down in the café."

We both sat on the sofa facing Phyllis.

"How are you doing?" he asked her gently.

She sniffled. "Okay I guess." And then she shook her head and dabbed at her face with a tissue to blot the newly formed tears. "Not really."

"I'm sorry," he said. "I came to tell you the guys with the new carpet just arrived. They told me they should be done by noon. So you can be home by this afternoon."

"Okay," she said with little enthusiasm. I'm sure the thought of returning to the scene of such a horrific event gave her very mixed emotions even though she claimed she was anxious to go back.

"I guess I need to start thinking about a funeral," she said. "I don't know where to begin."

"Ty and I will help you if you'd like. You might want to consider a memorial service. It's hard to know when the police might release his body."

The mention of "his body" started another crying jag. I suppose I could have couched it in softer terms but I didn't know what they could be. She was going to have to face reality sooner or later.

She finally quieted down. "I don't know any preachers in town. We haven't gone to church since we moved."

"We have a clergyman who's a resident here. Do you know Reverend Bill Michaels? He was with a nondenominational church. He's done services for several of our residents down in the multi-purpose room. They were quite nice."

I thought how handy it was to have a preacher in residence since the need for his services came up fairly often.

She looked down at her lap where she was twisting the damp tissue around her fingers.

"I don't know hardly anybody," she mumbled. "Justine Abnernathy is my only friend in this place. We used to know each other in Chapel Hill where we were neighbors. She's the reason we came here."

I was astonished she had any friends at GH. I was wondering why Justine hadn't made an effort to see Phyllis since Ralph's death.

"Would you like me to call Justine and ask her to come over? Maybe we all can help you plan a service."

"She left Monday for her sister-in-law's funeral in Connecticut. She won't be back until Sunday."

So probably she knew nothing of Ralph's death.

"Why don't we call Bill then," Ty said. "I'm sure he'd be more than happy to work with you planning a service, Phyllis."

"All right," she said.

I called Bill's apartment and was relieved to find him home. He said he would be right over.

The four of us spent the rest of the morning planning the details, or perhaps I should say the three of us with a little input from Phyllis now and then. She seemed incapable of pulling her thoughts together long enough to be of much help. When Bill questioned her about Ralph to put together a commentary on his life, she offered few details. I could tell Bill was going to have to pretty much wing it and use generic references to the deceased.

It was almost one o'clock when all the details were ironed out. The service would be held Monday afternoon at 3 pm downstairs in the multi-purpose room. I would arrange for flowers and Ty was going to contact Theresa Palmer, a long-time piano teacher who lives here, to provide the music. As far as finding anyone other than the Reverend Bill to eulogize Ralph, it probably wasn't going to happen. I think he'd pretty much ticked off most of the people around.

Phyllis didn't feel like going to the dining room for lunch so I scrabbled together a meal from cans of soup and a package of cheese that lasts forever and is edible only when it's hidden between slices of toasted bread. Bill declined the invitation to stay—can't say that I blame him— so the three of us ate mostly in silence. After we'd finished, Ty offered to check on Phyllis's apartment to see if the carpet installers were done, and Phyllis could go back home. I helped her fold up her clothes and put them in my tote, and when Ty returned with the good news her apartment was ready, accompanied her and Ty back to the east wing. Since her key was in her purse, she was able to get in now.

We met several people on the trek between the wings. They all seemed uneasy about encountering her and most of them averted their eyes. It was an uncomfortable situation for everyone. After all, what do you say to a woman accused of killing her husband? "So shocked to hear about his death?" "We're so sorry for your loss?" I'm sure they all wanted to ask her, "Why did you do it?"

Phyllis just kept her head down and ignored everyone.

The hall carpet no longer showed blood stains where the knife had lain. Apparently because of its dark print and the fact it was commercial grade, the maintenance staff had managed to clean it up. And the carpet was pristine white when we entered her apartment. But in my mind's eye I could still see the blood that had stained the white to a reddish black. I couldn't imagine what Phyllis was seeing. How would she ever get over the image of her husband covered in blood whether she was responsible or not?

I put away the clothes from the tote, changed the bed, and tidied up the bathroom. Ty was asking Phyllis if there were any errands he could run for her. She remembered that there was some medication that needed to be picked up at the drugstore so he went off to do that.

While we were waiting for Ty to return we chatted a little more. "Do you drive, Phyllis?" If Ralph had been the only driver in the family and ran all the errands, she was going to have to change her ways.

"I don't," she said. "I used to, but Ralph didn't think I was a safe driver so he wouldn't let me renew my license."

I wondered if Ralph had a legitimate reason or was simply trying to control her.

"Well, you know about the scheduled runs to the stores, don't you? It's all listed on your monthly calendar in the Glendon Hills newsletter. And you can ask our driver Ellen to take you to the doctor's. But if you need something that you can't get on one of those trips, give me a call and I'll take you." While my mouth was making the offer, my heart was leery that she might begin taking advantage and calling me all the time.

Ty was back shortly from the drugstore with the prescription. "Here you go, Phyllis. The druggist sent his condolences and said they'd be happy to deliver your medicine in the future."

"Thanks," she said. "Now if you don't mind, I think I'll lie down for a while."

That was the excuse we were looking for.

"Okay, Phyllis," I said. "Let us know if there's anything else we can do. Otherwise we'll see you at the service on Monday."

Ty and I left the apartment and went to the café. We both were emotionally exhausted from the past few days. I wanted a good strong cup of coffee and a chocolate chip cookie. Nothing like caffeine and chocolate to give one a lift. Ty settled for a diet coke. He always has such self control when it comes to calories. Makes me sick.

This was the first chance I had to tell him Phyllis's story about how she found Ralph dead when she came out of the bathroom.

"What do you think?" I asked when I'd given him all the details.

"About what?"

"Phyllis. Do you think she did it?"

"Hard to tell. It's hard to imagine her doing something like that. On the other hand, how could anyone have gotten in? That doesn't make sense. I really want to believe her, but it's obvious the cops don't."

"I know. That's what worries me. Seems like they made up their mind right from the start. Won't consider other scenarios."

"Well, let's hope Cliff can come up with something," Ty said.

"He'd better," I said brooding over my cup of coffee.

We both sat for a while without speaking, lost in thought.

"You know what Ty?"

"What?"

"We live here. We're in a position to check around, talk to people, maybe come up with some ideas on how it could have happened."

He looked at me skeptically. "Are you kidding? Don't you think you should leave that to the experts?"

"Well, frankly, I don't like how the experts are handling it. We live here and they don't. Maybe we're privy to information that they aren't."

"Like what?"

I scowled at him. "Oh, for heaven's sake, Ty, quit being such a spoil sport. Get with the program."

He shook his head. "Trouble with you is you don't have enough to occupy your mind these days. This is not a Girl Scout situation. This is real life with an ugly twist."

I stood up ready to walk away. "Okay. If that's the way you feel, I'll do it on my own."

He grabbed my arm and pulled me back down into my seat.

"You win, Vi-OH-la. I can't let you do this on your own. Who knows? It might be dangerous."

"You should know from dangerous," I said alluding to my suspicions he once was in the CIA.

He said nothing but winked at me.

CHAPTER EIGHT

Greta and Cliff came to the memorial service on Monday. The room was packed. It seemed as if every resident of GH was there. I'm sure it wasn't because of their fondness for Ralph, who was pretty much universally disliked, but out of curiosity. How was Phyllis going to react? Did she look like a cold-blooded killer?

I had to give her credit. She'd used makeup to make her pallor less visible, and wore a becoming dress in teal. She walked in with Justine at the last minute, holding her head high, to sit in the front row. Reverend Bill did a great job considering the paucity of information he had about Ralph. He managed to make a less-than-lovable man sound almost saintly, and I guess that's what memorial services are all about, to rehabilitate our imperfect selves.

Phyllis had decided not to have a reception after the service, and I totally understood why. It would have been very difficult to stand there accepting condolences from people who thought you were a murderer. So she and Justine left after the service was over. Many of the others stayed and stood around gossiping about the case I'm sure, but I didn't stick around to find out. I'd invited Greta and Cliff to stay for dinner, but it was only four o'clock so they came to my apartment, along with Ty, for a glass of wine.

Greta made over Sweetie as she always does when she visits. They have a dog who doesn't like cats so, although she's more of a cat lover than Cliff, they aren't able to have one much to her disappointment.

We talked about the service for a few minutes.

"I didn't get much of a sense of who Ralph was," Greta said. "The minister spoke in such generalities."

"That's because Phyllis wouldn't tell him anything." Ty said.

"Yes," said Cliff, "he does sound like a mystery man. I'm going to look into his background. See what I can find out about him."

"Did Phyllis tell you her side of the story?" I asked.

"About coming out of the bathroom to find Ralph dead on the floor? Of course. The police don't seem to buy that theory at all. Though it sounds pretty implausible, I certainly will look into it. But to tell the truth, I think my case will probably rely on her mental condition."

Oh god. I hated the sound of that. It could mean that she would be sent to a mental hospital if she was convicted.

"Don't you think there's a chance her story is true?"

Cliff rubbed his chin. "Maybe a slight chance. You can be sure I'll check it out, Vi. But I'm not optimistic. In the end I have to go with what I think will work best for her."

"Well," I said grasping at straws, "I wouldn't be surprised if she was abused." A defense of spousal abuse seemed better to me than one that would send her to an institution. With a sympathetic jury it might get her a not guilty verdict.

"I'll look into that as well, Vi. But what you have to understand is that I have to build my case on the scenario that has the best possible outcome."

"You mean even if you thought she was innocent you might use another defense?"

"If it's more likely to have the best results. It's tough, Vi, but you have to do whatever you think is best for your client."

I decided I'd said enough. Cliff wouldn't appreciate me trying to push him in a certain direction. I would quietly do what I had to do and not discuss it with anyone but Ty.

We went downstairs to the dining room and very carefully avoided the subject of Phyllis and Ralph. I was just as glad to have them out of my mind for an hour or so. I felt like I already was getting obsessed with the case.

Tuesday morning I went to the pool to swim. I'd missed some of my sessions the week before, and I wanted to get back in shape. The hour I spent in the pool was very restorative. As always I felt much better afterward, especially after spending ten minutes in the hot-tub/whirlpool, another of the wonderful perks here. My only disappointment was I have to follow the warning not to stay too long because it can raise blood pressure. Damned old age!

I try to join the pool exercise group when I can though I hadn't made it since Ralph's death. I'm always amazed at the number of women who refuse to go because they don't want to be seen in a bathing suit. That is so silly. At our age, all of us have unsightly bumps and lumps, but so what? We're all in the same boat. When do we get to the point we're no longer so uptight about our appearance? For a lot of people I guess the answer is never.

At lunchtime I told Ty I was going to call Justine and see if I could talk to her. I wanted to find out more about the Duncans' relationship.

"Do you want to join me?" I asked.

"No, you go on. She'd no doubt feel more comfortable talking to you alone than she would with a man around. She'll probably open up more."

I looked at him askance. "That's not an excuse is it? You aren't trying to wiggle out of this are you?"

He put on a look of pretend shock. "Would I mislead you, my dear? Of course not." Then he laughed. "No, I'm serious about that. Besides, I have an appointment to get my car serviced."

"Again?"

"Again. She takes a lot of loving care. But she's worth it."

With guys the cars always come first. But he had a point. Justine probably would be more comfortable with me alone. If she would talk to me at all.

I called her as soon as I got back to the apartment. I made it sound like my goal was to find out how I could help Phyllis adjust to widowhood.

"Sure, come on over," she said.

Justine lived on the second floor of the East Wing, two floors below Ty and Phyllis. She was a heavyset woman with dyed black hair, and her eyebrows had been completely plucked out with pencil-thin lines drawn in perfect curves in their place. She had a sweet, unlined face that had been transformed into a comic one by a bright red bow-shaped mouth that didn't follow the lines of her own thin lips and dots of too-red rouge on her cheekbones.

Her apartment was furnished with overstuffed, flower-bedecked furniture that seemed to suck up all the space and light in the living room. Every flat surface was covered with mementoes ranging from somewhat interesting to downright tacky. The heavy satin drapes covered most of the lovely view out her window that overlooked the woods.

I wanted to lead up to the subject at hand gradually. So I asked about her sister-in-law. "I understand you lost a relative last week. I'm so sorry."

"My brother's wife," she said. "They lived in Virginia, but we've always been close. It was rather unexpected."

"Is your brother doing all right?"

"He's taking it hard. You know how helpless men are when their wives die."

I just nodded. I'd seen that happen here at Glendon Hills. The women, though grieving, in general seem to handle the loss of a spouse better than the men.

"Well, on the same subject, I'm concerned about Phyllis," I said. "I don't know her well at all, but this has to be a difficult time for her. I got the impression she leaned on Ralph a lot. I'm sure it's going to be hard to manage on her own."

Justine chewed on her lip for a minute deep in thought. I got the impression she was deciding whether or not to confide in me.

Finally she said, "It wasn't so much she depended on him. He ruled the roost. It was his way or no way. This was a second marriage for them both since they'd both been divorced. Phyllis is the kind of woman who feels she has to have a man and that she can't function alone. She knuckled under to keep the peace. She just needed somebody--anybody."

"How long have you known her?"

"Oh, gosh, about ten years I guess. I moved next door to her when I got my divorce. She was single at the time, but quite unhappy about it. I kept trying to tell her singlehood wasn't all bad, but she wouldn't listen. Finally she met Ralph through a dating service, and it wasn't long before they were married. He moved in with her. Claimed his place was too small for them both. I think he was looking to freeload."

"Does she have a lot of money?"

"She doesn't have tons of it, but enough to be quite comfortable. It was from an inheritance. Ralph was a salesman, but not a particularly successful one. He was awfully abrasive."

"I was wondering why she didn't participate in activities around here. I don't think anyone really knew her. With the exception of you, of course."

"I think it was because Ralph embarrassed her. She was made very uncomfortable by his exasperating behavior when they were with other people. And frankly he was so controlling I don't think she wanted other people to witness her submissiveness. "

"It's got to make you wonder why she stayed with him."

"She told me she simply couldn't face going through another divorce or admit to herself she made a mistake. And I think she was afraid of him. She never actually told me he abused her, but I'm pretty sure he did."

I was thinking that killing him would have eliminated the need for a divorce. And then I mentally chastised myself for such an uncharitable thought. If she'd wanted to knock him off, she could have done it in a much less incriminating way.

Justine popped up from her chair. "Oh, goodness, I'm a terrible hostess. I didn't offer you a thing. Would you like tea or water? I have some delicious cookies."

I can't resist when someone offers me cookies. Maybe it is because of all those years of Girl Scout cookie sales. And it would give me a minute to think about how to ask her the next questions. "You know, tea would be great. And a cookie, too."

By the time she got back with a tray which she set on the coffee table, I was ready to go on. While I sipped my tea I asked, "I'm sure Phyllis has told you what happened on Tuesday. And I assume you know what the police are claiming happened. What's your take on this?"

She was taking a sip of tea and almost choked on it. She coughed as she set her glass back down on the tray and had to wait a few seconds before she could speak. "I don't think there's any way Phyllis would do anything like that!" Justine was quite worked up. Then she was quiet for a minute before she added, "Unless it got to the point she simply couldn't take it any more." She shook her head. "I don't know. I just don't know. Poor, poor Phyllis." A trickle of a tear ran down her cheek.

CHAPTER NINE

At dinner that evening I told Ty about my conversation with Justine. "At first she was adamant that Phyllis couldn't have done it. Then after she thought about it, she admitted the possibility that Ralph could have pushed her over the edge," I said. "She couldn't verify there was abuse but she seemed pretty sure of it."

"Ouch, that's not too helpful. Though it might be her best defense."

I nodded and took a bite of chicken tetrazzini. "Well, yes, I guess so."

"Whatever, her opinion isn't going to sway the district attorney I'm sure. I say we need to look into this further."

"Okay, how do you suggest we do that?" I asked.

"We have to find out more about both of them. Look into their past."

"Well, you're the research guy." Whenever I have a question about anything, Ty can usually find the answer, mostly through his computer. Though I have a computer too, I use it mainly for email to keep in touch with friends in distant places. I've never really gotten into researching via the internet.

That evening a local barbershop quartet was giving a concert in the multi-purpose room. We both love barbershop, Ty has a voice good enough he could have been a member. My singing voice sounds more like the losers on *American Idol*, but it doesn't diminish my love of music. Surprisingly, my mother's inept attempts at playing the viola managed to encourage my interest rather than ruin it for me. It's amazing the number of area musicians willing to come and entertain us. It was a pleasant interlude that took our minds off of the perplexing facts surrounding Ralph's death.

The next morning Ty met me in the café for coffee before exercise class.

"I had the strangest message on my phone when I got home last night," Ty said as he pumped himself a cup out of the big coffee dispenser on the counter. "A guy by the name of Perry Richards said he found me via the internet and he was some kind of a cousin to me. Never heard of the guy. But he'll be in town this week and wants to meet me."

"So you're not the only one doing research on the net," I said.

"Heck, no. Everybody does it. But it could very well be some sort of a scam. We'll just have to wait and see."

Ty had the soul of a skeptic so it didn't surprise me he was leery of the call. I thought it was kind of exciting to think he might have a long-lost relative.

"Anyway, I did have a chance to do a little checking myself and found out a couple of places where Ralph worked when he lived in Chapel Hill. Would you like to go over there this afternoon and see what we can find out about him?"

"Of course. I'm more curious about him than ever after talking to Justine."

"Why don't we leave right after exercise class so we'll get there in time to eat at A Southern Season."

"Give me a chance to shower first. I don't want to wear my grungy exercise clothes to interview people."

He looked me up and down, taking in my ancient bright blue polyester running suit. "You look okay to me."

"That's what I love about you. You're so nonjudgmental. At least about some things."

After exercise class Spunky came up to us. She waited till everyone else had left before she spoke.

"Isn't it tragic about Phyllis and Ralph?" she said. "I understand you two were the ones who saw her right after it happened."

"Yes, we were on the way to Ginger's place to console her about losing her bird," I said.

Spunky made a funny little face. She would never speak ill of any resident, but I knew she too had been subjected to Lester's vocabulary. "Yes, poor Ginger as well," she said charitably.

"Not quite in the same category," Ty added.

Spunky said nothing but shook her head and shrugged. "Do you know how Phyllis is doing?" she asked.

"Not so well," I said. "You can imagine how she feels with a possible trial looming over her."

"Actually I can't imagine it. It's beyond my comprehension. I don't know Phyllis well. You're aware of how much she's kept to herself. But when they first moved in, I went to their place to introduce myself. Ralph happened to be gone at the time, and Phyllis and I had a good little talk. In fact she pretty much unburdened her soul to me. I was rather taken aback. But I guess she felt she had to let off steam."

Ty and I looked at each other. Maybe Spunky had some information we didn't know.

I decided to fill her in. "Ty and I feel that Phyllis has been railroaded by the cops. She told us she found Ralph dead on the living room floor when she came out of the bathroom, and the knife was on the floor beside him. She was afraid the killer was still in the apartment, so she picked up the knife to defend herself then ran into the hall."

"Why don't they believe her?" Spunky asked looking shocked.

"Because they claim no one could have gotten into their locked apartment. Everyone who had a pass key had an alibi."

"Why didn't Phyllis just claim she'd forgotten to lock the door the night before?"

"Because she's too honest," I said. "When they asked her about the door I doubt she even thought about saying anything else. I don't think it even occurred to her to lie in order to exonerate herself."

"It's going to get to the point we're going to have to put surveillance cameras in all the halls. Whoever thought something like this could happen here?" Spunky asked.

"Did Phyllis say anything to you that could help us?" Ty asked. "Vi and I have decided to become proactive and try to find some answers about why this happened. There's got to be more to it than the cops think there is."

"Possibly. I remember her saying that they'd moved here because Ralph had made some people so angry he decided it would be best to move away. Her best friend, Justine, was living here and suggested to them that they come."

"Was she any more specific than that?" I asked. "Who was mad at him?"

"She mentioned arguments with former coworkers."

"Say, Spunky," Ty said, "could you get us her former address? We'd already planned to go to Chapel Hill today, and it might be a good idea to interview former neighbors. If you've got it handy it would save me having to search the net."

She smiled like a conspirator. "I think I can do that for you. Probably shouldn't, but I don't see what it could hurt."

We followed her to her office which was located between the swimming pool and workout room where she had all kinds of resident information on her computer. It only took her a couple of minutes to bring it up. She wrote the address on a piece of paper and handed it to Ty.

"Mum's the word," she said.

I put my fingers to my lips and twisted the invisible key as I did as a child when I wanted to show I could keep a secret.

After showering and changing into a pair of black slacks and a long-sleeved tee in a paisley print, I met Ty in the lobby. He had changed into dark gray slacks and a pale blue dress shirt unbuttoned at the neck. I guess he decided he needed to look a little more business-like to interview people.

When we got to his car, he opened the trunk and pulled out a small bag. "This is for you," he said. "If you're going to keep riding around with me in this buggy I thought you would need this."

It was a pink sequined ball cap. Since he loved driving with the top down, the cap would help keep my hair from blowing in my face. He always wore his own baby blue cap with a UNC logo on it.

"Thank you, Ty," I said. "It even matches my top." I pointed to splashes of pink in the multi-colored top.

"You look quite spiffy," he said as I put it on. I looked in the mirror under the visor and decided I did indeed look spiffy.

It was a beautiful day for a drive. The interstate was lined with redbud and a little further back into the woods the dogwood was now in full bloom. We were in Chapel Hill in a little over an hour and went directly to A Southern Season in the University Mall. It's a destination that attracts visitors from all over: a large store filled with all kinds of wonderful things to eat, many of them North Carolina specialties like cheese straws, Moravian cookies, and North Carolina barbeque. It also features dinnerware, glassware, and a huge wine selection. It's a lot of fun just to wander around and admire all the goodies, but we didn't have time today so we ate in their adjoining restaurant. Afterward we couldn't get out of the store without at least buying some cheese straws.

With full stomachs, we headed out to visit some of the places where we knew Ralph Duncan had worked.

The first was Fantana Fencing Company located on Route 15-501 south of town. Ty pulled into the parking lot, and we went into the sales showroom. A middle-aged man with unruly salt-and-pepper hair and beard stood hunched over behind the counter scrutinizing his computer screen. He looked up as we came in the door.

"May I help you?" The man smiled broadly.

"I hope so," Ty answered. "I'm here about a former employee."

"Oh, and who is that?" the man asked.

"Ralph Duncan."

It looked as though a storm cloud passed across the man's features. "Is he applying for a job somewhere?"

"No," I piped up. "Look, would it be possible to talk to you privately?"

The man hesitated for a minute. Then he went to a door behind the counter and opened it. "Joe, come here will you?" he hollered into a back room.

A young man who looked like a Harvard business school graduate came hurrying out. He probably lost a middle management job and was glad to find any work at all.

"Take my place here while I take these people to my office." He motioned us to follow him, and we trailed him to another door which led into a small, cluttered office. There was a big old oak swivel chair behind a desk covered with stacks of paperwork, and one small plastic lawn chair in front of it. Ty signaled for me to sit in the plastic one as our guide settled into his chair. "Sorry," he said to Ty.

"No problem," he answered. "I've been sitting most of the morning."

"And you are...? The man asked.

"I'm Viola Weatherspoon," I said.

"Ty Landowski."

"I'm Ray Fantana. Owner of this place. Now why on earth do you want to know about that good-for-nothing Ralph Duncan?"

"Ralph is dead." Ty said.

Ray's eyes opened wide in shock. Then he said, "I'll bet it wasn't a natural death."

"Why do you say that?" I asked.

"Because he screwed over too many people. How did it happen?"

"He and his wife have been living in a retirement center in Guilford City. A little over a week ago he was stabbed to death in his apartment," Ty said.

"My god," Ray said. "In a retirement center? That must have gotten the codgers' panties in a twist."

I sat up straight in my chair and glared at him. "We are not *codgers*, Mr. Fantana. We happen to live there too. We are active older adults." We can call ourselves geezers or whatever, but everybody else better watch their mouth.

His face turned scarlet. "Um, sorry," he murmured. "Didn't mean to insult you."

Ty gave me a quick look that said *good for you, kiddo.*

"The thing is," I continued, "his wife has been charged with his murder. But we don't think she did it."

"I never met her," Ray said, "But I wondered how he ever conned anyone into marrying him. They got married just before he started working here. I heard on the grapevine that she had some money, so I always figured that was his motive for wanting to get hitched."

"So we want to know more about him. Why do you have such a low opinion of him?" Ty asked.

"He was screwing our customers," Ray said. Then he looked at me and began to blush again. "Uh, sorry for the language."

"That doesn't bother me a bit," I said. "Just don't insult us."

He looked chastised. I decided not to get on his case again for fear of preventing him from telling us what we wanted to know.

"How did he do that?" Ty asked.

"He inflated the quotes for fencing and would pocket the difference between what it actually cost and what he charged the customer. He got away with it for a while before I realized what was going on."

"How did you find out?" Ty was now leaning against a metal file cabinet. I suspected his back was beginning to bother him as it commonly did when he stood for a while.

"One of our other salesmen went back to check on a job while Ralph was on vacation. When he found out what Ralph had charged them, he flipped. He didn't dare tell the customer, but he told me."

"So why didn't you turn it over to the cops?" I asked.

"I didn't want to wreck my good name. I quietly reimbursed the customer the difference. I went back through the records and found several other customers he'd bilked, so I reimbursed them as well. It cost me a bundle, but it preserved my reputation."

"So you fired Ralph and that was it?"

"Yeah. I withheld his last paycheck and didn't pay him his accumulated vacation and sick time to recoup a smidgen of what I lost. I hoped he'd learned a lesson."

"I kind of doubt it. He got a job selling used cars when he left here." Ty said.

Ray shook his head. "Oh, no. I thought maybe he'd live off his wife's money, but I guess that wasn't enough for him."

"Any of your employees have a particular grudge against him?" I thought it would be worthwhile to explore that avenue.

"There was a guy, name of Ed Stillman. He quit not long after I fired Ralph. It seems Ralph stole some customers from Ed. People would call in for prices, and Ed would talk to them on the phone and tell them they were only ballpark quotes. Of course you can't give a fixed quote till you go out and measure the property. Occasionally people would say they wanted to think it over. Then when they'd call back and ask for Ed and Ed was out, Ralph would tell them he was taking on the job for Ed. And of course he always jacked up the price Ed had quoted and pocketed the difference. He managed to keep Ed from seeing the paperwork until just before I fired him. Ed was furious. In fact he quit over it."

"Where's Ed now?" I asked.

"Not sure."

"Anything else you can tell us?" Ty asked.

Ray thought for a minute. "Don't think so. But why do they think his wife killed Ralph anyway?"

"We found her standing in the hall with the knife that killed him in her hand."

"Well, I don't know the lady, but I can see how he might have driven her to it. What a shame though."

"We're pretty sure she didn't do it," I said. "That's why we're looking into Ralph's past."

"Well, good luck on that," Ray said.

CHAPTER TEN

We didn't have much to say to each other when we left Fantana Fencing. Our meeting with Ray only confirmed what we thought about Ralph Duncan. He was not a nice guy. We drove back up 15-501 to the north side of town to George Grant's Foreign Auto Sales. A large lot displayed dozens of cars in all sizes, shapes, and colors gleaming under rows of colored banners and bright lights. Ty's face lit up like a kid's as we drove into it. Surrounded by all of these imported cars from fancy little sport coupes to big luxurious sedans, he seemed to be in a state of nirvana. I wondered if he could concentrate on the task at hand without being distracted by all the manly goodies on display.

We no sooner got out of the car but we were met by a salesman, a tall thin man with combed back hair and sleek mustache.

"I see you're a gentleman who appreciates fine sports cars," he said almost bowing. Ty's car had been purchased second hand and wasn't one of the pricey ones to begin with, but the salesman knew how to stroke his ego.

"Yeah, I'm kind of fond of my set of wheels," Ty replied.

The salesman offered his hand. "Clark Lassiter," he said.

Ty shook his hand. "Ty Landowski," he said, "and my friend Vi Weatherspoon."

Clark beamed his practiced smile. "You wanting to trade in this baby?"

"'Fraid not," Ty said. "I'm here to inquire about a former salesman."

The smile disappeared.

"How long ago was he here?"

"I think he left a year or so ago."

"You'll have to talk to the owner then. I've only been here six months. Follow me." Clark seemed a lot less friendly now that he knew we weren't here to buy a car. Oh well, I knew times were tough and car sales were slow. He had a right to be disappointed.

Clark took us inside to an office directly off the big open showroom full of sport convertibles. Ty looked at them longingly. I could tell he was having a hard time not being able to linger a while to check them out.

In the office George Grant greeted us politely and gestured for us to sit in the chairs facing him. Ty went through the formalities of introducing us.

"And how can I help you?" he asked.

"We're trying to find information on a former salesman of yours." Ty said.

"Oh? Who might that be?"

"Ralph Duncan"

We got the same reaction that we'd gotten from Ray Fantana. Ralph certainly hadn't left good vibes wherever he went.

George scowled and pressed his lips into a thin line. He seemed to be working hard to control what he wanted to say about Ralph. "And why do you want to know about him?"

"He was killed last week," I offered.

"Traffic accident?"

"No. Stabbed to death."

He hesitated a moment to take that in. But he didn't seem overly shocked. "Here in Chapel Hill? I didn't see anything about it."

"No, in Guilford City where he was living in a retirement center."

"What happened?"

Ty gave him the short version of Ralph's demise. He didn't mention Phyllis's arrest. I guess he wanted to see what George's reaction would be.

"Unbelievable!" George exclaimed. "How's Phyllis doing? Was she still married to him?"

"You knew her?" I asked.

"Well, yeah. She came to plead with me to keep him on when I had to give Ralph the boot. I felt really sorry for her, but I told her there was nothing I could do. The guy was a crook."

"What did you think of her?" I asked.

"She seemed like a really nice lady. Couldn't figure how she got up with the likes of Ralph, but there's no accounting for tastes. I think she wanted him to keep the job so he'd be away from the house all day."

"What made you think that?" Ty asked.

"Just a gut feeling from the way she talked."

"What would you think if I told you Phyllis has been charged with his murder?"

"I would think he probably drove her to it."

"You met her," I said. "Do you really think she's capable of such a thing?"

"Well, when you put it that way, I'd have a hard time believing it. But people do surprise you sometimes."

Not the answer I wanted, but I could tell he had his doubts.

"Can you tell us why you had to fire him?" Ty asked.

"He had ways of inflating the prices without my knowledge and pocketing the difference. Took me a while to find out. He got into a fight with another salesman out behind the service building and hurt him pretty bad. That's really why I canned him. And then I found out what he'd been doing."

"Would you give us the name of the guy he fought with?" Ty asked.

He scowled. "Why? That was a while back."

"Because anything we can find out about his past might help Phyllis," I said. "We feel strongly she's being railroaded on this. So we want to check into other possibilities."

"Well," George paused, "I guess it can't hurt. But he quit a few months ago and I don't know where he is now."

"There are ways to find him," Ty said. I wondered if he had ways I didn't know about.

"His name was Farley Lathrop. Hated to lose him. He was a damn good salesman."

We thanked George and left the office. Ty couldn't help but linger about the showroom and check out the cars that beckoned with their sexy lines and expensive upholstery. Clark strode over and began to point out the finer points of each one extolling their horsepower and comfort and extraordinary accessories. I never heard a thing about gas mileage. It was another forty-five minutes before Ty had his fill and reluctantly returned to his own car.

"You aren't really thinking about buying a new one, are you?" I asked as I plopped into the low seat in a less than lady-like fashion and got my ball cap off the shift stick where I'd hung it.

"Oh, no. I love this girl." He patted the steering wheel. "You like to window shop don't you?"

"Not so much." I never was much of a shopper. Maybe it's because I don't have the sylph-like figure that makes clothes shopping enjoyable. And for me house decorating only means finding a comfortable sofa and chair and tables to hold lamps. None of this HGTV stuff.

He grinned at me. "Well, I've always known you're unique, Vi. Maybe what appeals to me is that you're not such a girly girl."

I didn't know whether to feel complimented or insulted. "Where next?" I asked rather than comment.

He looked at his watch. "Why don't we call it a day. If we leave now we'll get back in time to have an early dinner. Besides, his former neighbors probably all are working stiffs. I think we'd have a better chance of finding them home on Saturday."

"Okay by me."

As we drove toward Interstate 40 west to head back to Guilford City I asked Ty, "Do you think we made any headway today?"

He shrugged. "We've got the names of a couple of guys who probably hated Ralph's guts. The only thing is why would they wait till now to have their revenge? Especially the guy from the fencing company. That's been several years."

"Sometimes past grudges can grow and grow inside your head, especially if you're going through hard times now. With the recession and people out of work, maybe all they can think about is getting back at somebody who did them wrong even if it was well in the past."

"Something to consider," Ty said as he passed a big minivan full of old ladies and gave a toot of the horn and little wave. They all waved back.

CHAPTER ELEVEN

We got back to GH a little before five when the dining room doors open. As we passed the reception desk, Patricia waved us over.

"That man over there on the far sofa?" she inclined her head in his direction. "He says he's a relative of yours."

Every non-resident who enters has to sign in at the front desk and state who they are visiting. They are pretty careful about security around here, and not just since Ralph's death. Back doors open to additional parking lots but it takes a key card to open them.

Ty scowled but said nothing. He took my elbow and said, "Let's go see who this guy is."

When we approached him he jumped up and threw out his arms as if to embrace us both at once. "Tyrone? Is that you?"

He was a heavy-set fellow with only a fringe of hair around a shiny red and peeling scalp. His ears stuck out slightly and his nose was bulbous. In other words he looked nothing at all like Ty.

Ty stepped back to avoid his embrace. "You're Perry I assume." There was little warmth in his voice.

Perry brought his arms back to his sides but seemed unfazed. "Yes, yes, of course. And who is this lovely lady?"

"I'm Viola Weatherspoon," I said. "I'm also a resident here."

Perry grinned what he probably thought was a conspiratorial grin and nodded. "Oh, yes, I see."

"No, you don't see," Ty said stonily. I'd never seen him act so unfriendly before. Something about this guy seemed to really turn him off. "Is there some reason you've come here?" He wasn't about to beat about the bush with niceties.

Perry smiled again. "I've gotten into this genealogy thing. Went to this website that finds your ancestors and found that you were my second cousin. I decided I had to look you up. Isn't it a shame we didn't know about each other all these years?"

From the look on Ty's face I don't think he felt it was a bad thing at all.

"And just how is it we're related?" he asked.

"Your grandfather on your mother's side was a half brother to my grandmother on my father's side. Simple really."

Ty glanced at his watch. "I'd like to have that spelled out to me. Exactly who is who."

"Sure," Perry grinned again. "I've got the family tree I copied from the website out in my car. I'd love to go over it with you."

"We were going in to dinner. Would you like to join us?" I asked. I knew Ty was never going to ask him, and I decided the best thing to do was to feed Perry and send him on his way.

"Great," Perry said. "Let me run out to my car and get the family tree. We can look at it during the meal." He scurried off to the parking lot.

"Why did you do that?" Ty was angry. "I wanted to get rid of him."

"For heavens sake, let the poor man have his say. It won't hurt you to listen."

"I'm sure it's some kind of a scam. He wants something from me, I can tell."

"So what would keep you from saying no? It's as simple as that."

Ty frowned and folded his arms across his chest in a defensive position. "You know what? This guy reminds me of Ralph Duncan. Same kind of obnoxious personality. I can smell a shyster a mile away."

"Don't you think that's a snap judgment? Give the guy a chance, Ty."

He just glowered. You'd think we were an old married couple the way we were acting.

Perry was back in a few minutes carrying a small briefcase. Ty said nothing but turned and walked to the dining room leaving us to follow. He asked for a table in the far corner where we could have some privacy.

Perry chattered on about how nice the amenities were at Glendon Hills as we waited for our dinners. Ty said nothing but drew crisscross lines in the tablecloth with the tines of his fork. He wasn't going to do a thing to make Perry feel comfortable so I tried my best. I found his personality fairly abrasive, too, but I didn't think that called for rudeness. I knew that Ty's behavior stemmed from the fact that he'd been conned in the past, though he never told me the details, which made him wary of anyone who seemed to be trying too hard to worm his way into his good graces.

Finally our meals arrived. Perry carried on excessively about the high quality of the food. I thought I could see the wheels turning in his mind that Ty must be fairly wealthy to be living in such a nice place. I felt sure money was the basis for this visit. The truth is you don't have to be rich. It isn't the least expensive place in town, but with a decent pension, social security, and funds from selling a house, it's possible for middle-income seniors to live here.

After we finished dessert and the plates were cleared away, Perry opened his briefcase and spread some papers on the table. Ty and I were sitting across from him so he positioned the pages so we could read them. There was a rather fancy family tree in full color that had the different generations imprinted on the limbs. Perry carefully pointed out the relationships to Ty going back beyond the two generations that connected them. He seemed quite excited about the whole idea of genealogy.

"So you see," he concluded pointing at the names on the tree, "when you come down two generations on each side that makes us second cousins. But if we look at my father, he would be your first cousin once removed."

"You say your grandmother was only a half sister to Ty's grandfather. Does it still work with half siblings?" I asked. I knew the answer but was trying desperately to keep some conversation going.

"Of course. My grandmother's mother died when my grandmother was only nine so her father married again. And Tyrone's grandfather came from that union. But at least half of the genes that link us are still there."

Ty finally spoke. "Okay, so we're related. I see that. Thanks for coming by, Perry." He brushed his lips with his napkin, folded it neatly, laid it on the table, and began to rise.

Perry stood up too. "Tyrone, I know you're busy and have things to do, but could I please ask for an hour or so of your time this evening? In private?" He looked at me apologetically.

Oh, god, I thought, here comes the pitch. I wondered if Ty was going to take him by the scruff of the neck and escort him out the front door. I hoped he wouldn't make a scene.

Ty stood completely still for a minute without saying anything. Finally he sighed a deep sigh and glanced at his watch. "Okay, Perry. I'll give you one hour but no longer. Come on, we'll go up to my apartment."

Perry nodded deferentially and hurriedly shoved the papers back into the briefcase. He put out his hand to shake mine. "So nice to meet you, Viola. I do hope we have a chance to meet again."

Looking at Ty's face I thought *that's not likely*. But I clasped his hand and mentally wished him well this next hour. I didn't know if Ty was taking him upstairs to read him the riot act or what.

And so the two men went off to the East Wing while I retired to the West. It had been a long day and I was tired. I was very happy I had not been included in the meeting as it was bound to be contentious. So I went home, put on my jammies and watched TV before going to bed early.

CHAPTER TWELVE

The next morning I went to the pool early to swim my laps. I was dying of curiosity about what went on in Ty's apartment the night before, but knew he would call me in due time and fill me in. At least I hoped he would. I was afraid he might be angry with me for inviting Perry to dinner and pretty much forcing the later confrontation or whatever it had turned out to be. I just hoped he wasn't too hard on the poor man. He did seem like something of a loser.

I hadn't been back in my apartment long when Ty called.

"May I come over and talk to you?" he asked.

"Sure." So he was still speaking to me at least.

I put a pot of coffee on while I waited for him.

When he rang my doorbell, I opened the door to find him standing there with a troubled look on his face.

Before I sat down I asked him if he wanted a cup of coffee.

"Yeah. Sure," he said. He sounded despondent.

I filled two cups and carried them into the living room and handed one to him. He sat dejectedly on the sofa and looked like he had the weight of the world on his shoulders. He was staring at the floor.

I sat down in the chair across from him and sipped my coffee as I waited for him to speak. Normally I would have said something flippant to get the conversation started, but I could tell from his expression that it wouldn't be appropriate this time.

Finally he looked up at me. "Well, Perry wanted something all right," he said.

"Money?"

"No, not money. He wants a kidney."

I was so shocked I didn't know what to say.

"Perry's been on dialysis for some time. He'll be on it for the rest of his life if he doesn't get a transplant, and his health is deteriorating pretty rapidly in the meantime."

"So why did he come to you?"

"They haven't been able to find a good match for him yet. He doesn't have any immediate family so he got the idea of trying to find a relative on line hoping they might be a match."

"Well, just because you're distantly related doesn't necessarily mean you're a match does it?"

"No. But he feels he's running out of options so this is kind of his last chance."

We both sat in silence for a while.

"I checked him out on the internet after he left," Ty said. "He has a history of scrapes with the law. When he was young he got busted for things like disorderly conduct and public drunkenness. He was arrested a few years back for receiving stolen goods. He actually spent a couple of years in jail in Virginia but finally got out on parole. It seems he's been on the straight and narrow since, but that's probably because of his health. He doesn't have the time or energy to get in trouble now."

"Oh, Ty," I said. "That's sad."

"Didn't expect to find someone like that in my family. But I guess every family has its black sheep."

"So what are you going to do?"

"I wish I knew, Vi. The guy is such a loser."

"But should that make a difference?"

He shook his head. "I don't know, Vi. I hardly slept all night. Perry is asking me to put my life on the line to help save his. It isn't exactly like he's my brother or someone I care about."

"Is the operation really that dangerous?"

"Well, no, not normally. But any operation can go awry. Do I owe him anything? What has he contributed to the good of mankind?"

"Maybe you're not a match, Ty. Why don't you check it out? If it turns out you're not that would settle it once and for all."

"Yeah, but if it turns out I am a match, he'd never leave me alone until I consented to the operation."

"So I ask you again: what are you going to do?"

"I wish to hell I knew."

I felt really sorry for Ty. He seemed to be going through some kind of existential crisis, and there was nothing I could do to help him.

He went off to play cards with the Dudes, hoping, I'm sure, to take his mind off Perry for a while.

I decided to visit Phyllis. I hadn't seen her since the memorial service on Monday and didn't have a chance to talk to her then. I called her first and asked if it was all right to come. She said she'd be happy to see me.

When I got to her apartment, Justine was there.

"Justine just dropped by," Phyllis said. "She's been so good to me since...well, you know what. I don't know what I'd do without her."

We greeted each other, and I joined them in the living room.

"I wanted to see if there was anything I can do for you, Phyllis," I said. "I'm never sure what people need until they tell me what would be helpful. Some people instinctively know to do the right thing, but you have to point me in the right direction."

"That's not so, Vi. You and Ty were so wonderful the day it happened and after I came home from the hospital. I'll never forget that."

"I'm just glad we happened to be there."

"Me too," Justine chimed in. "I still feel bad I was gone and wasn't here to help Phyllis." She said. "I'm trying to make up for it now. I just brought her a coffee cake I got at the Sweet Shoppe. How about a piece?"

How could I refuse? Sweets are my downfall.

Justine brought me a large piece along with another cup of coffee. I was going to be flying high from caffeine any moment now.

I'd been debating whether I should mention our trip to Chapel Hill. I finally decided I might as well. Phyllis could probably add more information to what we'd already learned.

"Phyllis," I said, "I want you to know that Ty and I went to Chapel Hill yesterday to talk to some of the people Ralph used to work for."

"Oh," she said looking surprised. "Why did you do that?"

"We just wanted to learn a little more about Ralph. Now please don't say anything to Cliff about this. I don't think he'd appreciate our efforts."

She bit her lip and frowned. "You're not getting me into any more trouble are you?"

"Oh, lord, no, Phyllis. We're trying to help you. We found out that Ralph made some enemies along the way. Maybe that can help your case."

"You think so?"

"It seems there could be people out there who might have been holding grudges against him even though he knew them some years ago. You never can tell what will set some people off. Maybe the bad economy has hurt them, and they feel like they can trace their bad luck back to Ralph. Who knows what goes through people's minds?"

Phyllis wrung her hands and seemed quite distressed. "I didn't know these things about Ralph until after we were married. He seemed so different when we were dating."

Justine reached over and patted her knee. "You got taken in by him, honey. He married you because he thought you were rich."

Phyllis broke down at this and began crying copiously. "I messed up the first time around. I really wanted this marriage to work. But I couldn't do anything to please him."

Justine looked at me and shook her head sadly.

I waited till she calmed down. Then I asked Phyllis if she knew George Grant.

She pulled several tissues from the box beside her on the table and wiped her eyes and nose. Then she nodded. "He owns the car lot."

"We talked to him. He told us that when he fired Ralph, you begged him to keep him on."

This brought on another round of tears. "Yes," she gulped. "I knew my life would be miserable if he was home all day. He took his frustrations out on me."

"Then why were you willing to move to Glendon Hills with him?" I asked, a little more impatiently than I meant to. "Why didn't you just move away?"

"I...I'm not sure. I guess I'm a sucker. He promised to turn over a new leaf and be a better person. I wanted to believe him. And I thought if I lived in a place like this full of people, he'd have to treat me well. People would know if he didn't."

"And did he turn over that leaf?"

She lowered her head in shame. "No, he didn't. He still kept me under his thumb."

Now I was feeling guilty. "I'm ashamed to say I didn't realize it, Phyllis. I always thought it was your choice to stay in your apartment all the time. I thought you were just very shy."

Justine spoke up. "I should have insisted she participate more in activities around here. I'm sorry too for letting things go on like that."

"One last question. Did you ever meet Farley Lathrop?" I asked when Phyllis had calmed down a bit.

"I don't think so," Phyllis replied. "Who is he?"

"He had a fist fight with Ralph just before Ralph got fired. I understand he was pretty bitter about it. But I don't know what it was about."

"Ralph never mentioned him."

I'd upset her enough so I changed the subject to talk about some of the violent weather that had occurred that week to the south of us. The storms that used to plague the Midwest seem to be moving eastward and threatening our area with their killer tornadoes. So we jumped from one unpleasant topic to another, but one that had no personal implications. That made it easier to talk about.

CHAPTER TWELVE

Ty and his buddies ordered sandwiches from the dining room and played through the dinner hour so I ate with some of the other residents. I knew that I should do this more often, but Ty and I feel so comfortable with each other that we generally opt to eat together. There's no pressure to make conversation for the sake of conversation or get into unpleasant discussions on politics. But I really enjoyed the company of several women that evening because I didn't have to dwell on all the troubling questions we'd been facing recently with Phyllis's situation and now Perry's request. It was fun to talk about movies and books and other non-confrontational subjects.

That evening they had scheduled a lecture in the multi-purpose room on John Muir, the naturalist, which seemed like a pleasant way to end the day. On the way out of the room when the talk was over I ran into Ginger Willard. With all the other things happening, I'd forgotten about her and her parrot.

We walked down the hall together toward the lobby.

"How are you, Ginger?" I asked.

"Oh, okay I guess. But I miss Lester so much."

"I'm sure you do. It takes time."

"I got a little bouquet of flowers today at the supermarket and put them on the grave. Just to let him know I'm thinking about him."

"That was sweet," I said, willing myself not to roll my eyes.

At the lobby we parted ways. She went off to the East Wing and I went back to my apartment. I was beginning to wonder if they'd put all the strange ones on the east side. Nobody on my hall quite measured up to Ginger and Phyllis for peculiarity.

The next morning while we were in the midst of our exercise class I began speculating about Ginger again. I decided her love for her trash-talking bird was motivated by the same thing that made Phyllis stay with Ralph: the need for companionship, no matter how lacking in geniality.

And then a disturbing thought occurred to me.

I couldn't wait until the class was over. As we walked out the door I said to Ty, "I have something I want to talk to you about."

He frowned. "Not Perry I hope."

This was the first time we'd been together since his revelation about Perry's request. We didn't meet for coffee before exercise because I overslept and barely made it to class.

"No, not all." I wasn't about to bring up that subject again. I'd wait until Ty was ready to talk about it.

"Let's go have coffee then."

As we sat in the café, I told him about the theory that had popped into my mind that morning.

"I got to thinking about Lester," I said. "Ginger told us that parrots can live into their fifties, but Lester was only about twenty-three."

"Right," Ty said. "So?"

"Well, I thought it was pretty strange that he hadn't shown any signs of sickness or anything. Just up and died."

"Okay. I'm sure you have a point here."

"I'm getting there," I said. "This crazy idea came into my head, but when you think about it, it makes sense. What if someone came onto your hall with the intention of killing Ralph Duncan. He probably had a pass key, don't you think?"

"Guess he'd have to."

"What if…" I paused for drama.

"Go on."

"What if he went into Ginger's place first by mistake. Then he noticed the bird, realized it was the wrong apartment, but Lester was waking up and starting to make a fuss. The guy panicked, afraid the bird would wake its owner, so he went to the cage, opened it and did something to Lester. Like broke his neck or something."

Ty took a long drink of coffee.

"My god, Vi, you have an active imagination."

"Well, maybe so. But if we found out that his neck *was* broken or he was physically hurt, wouldn't that pretty much prove someone was there who shouldn't have been?"

"I suppose so. Though I doubt it is enough to get Phyllis off the hook."

"But it might get them looking into other possibilities instead of deciding it had to be her."

"Okay, one question. How are you going to do this? The bird is buried out in the woods somewhere."

"I saw Ginger last night after the program. She told me she got a bouquet of flowers yesterday and put them on the grave. That should make it pretty easy to find."

"Ginger would have a fit if she knew someone was digging up her beloved bird."

"That's why I think we should wait till after dark. We dig it up, but put the dirt back with the flowers on top so it doesn't look disturbed. Then we take it to the all night vet's and see what they can tell us. Afterward, we can bury him again."

Ty leaned back in his chair and smiled. "Vi, you are something else. Did the Girl Scouts have a sleuthing badge?"

"No. But it might not be a bad idea."

That afternoon Ty went back to his bridge buddies, and I decided I'd take a lesson in Mah Jongg. I needed something other than exercise class and swimming and playing detective, especially an activity that would involve me with residents other than Ty and our two troubled women.

I enjoyed my hour in the game room. Mah Jongg was interesting and challenging, and I resolved to meet with the group each week from now on. But unfortunately that day I was quite distracted by thoughts of what we were going to do that evening.

After dinner Ty and I decided to go into the library and read magazines until it got dark. Since Daylight Saving Time hadn't yet started, it wasn't long before dusk fell, and we felt it was safe to go on out to the woods. We skulked around close to the edge of the building until we were well past the area where we might be seen from Ginger's window. I figured the grave had to be near the lawn because the undergrowth was pretty thick beneath the trees. We walked along just inside the forest's edge where we would be hidden from prying eyes in the building. In good sleuthing mode I'd reminded Ty to wear dark clothing and he complied. Even if he did make a sarcastic remark or two.

It took us about fifteen minutes to find the grave with the help of a penlight that I'd brought along. I figured it couldn't be seen from the building like the light from a regular flashlight would. I also carried a hand trowel. I'd hidden these items in a small bag that I'd taken into the dining room as if I were going to take leftovers back to my apartment. I'd brought the trowel from New York thinking I might do some gardening in the plot devoted to the residents out beyond the parking lot. I hadn't yet made the effort, but maybe I'd do it this year if only for some home grown tomatoes.

We never would have found the grave if it hadn't been for the bunch of daisies and Echinacea tied with a bow that was laid across the top. The stone she'd mentioned was beside it, but it wasn't distinctive enough that I would have realized it marked the spot. Ty removed the bouquet, and I started to dig with the trowel. I hit metal very quickly. I remembered she'd told us she'd buried Lester in a metal box and was grateful that she had. I imagine he would have been pretty badly decomposed otherwise. As it was, I didn't want to open the box and see what he looked like. I just hoped there was enough left that the vet could tell what happened to him. It only took a few minutes to dig it up, dust off the dirt, refill the hole, and place the flowers back where they'd been.

I placed the "casket" in a plastic grocery store bag, and we sneaked out of the woods, around the front of the building to Ty's car. The emergency vet office that was open at night was a couple of miles away on Southland Street. When we entered the lobby carrying a Food Lion bag with something square in the bottom, the receptionist must have wondered if we'd lost our minds. But she'd probably seen everything because she didn't blink an eye, just asked us why we were there.

"I have a dead parrot in here," I said, raising the bag to eye level. "I need to know why it died."

"So you want a necropsy," she said. "You realize it won't be cheap. Are you sure you want to do this?"

"Yes," I said. "I'm not the grieving owner so I'm not doing it because I'm upset. I need the answers for a very important reason."

She showed no curiosity about my reason. Perhaps she'd learned it's better not to know. "Okay. We'll be glad to do it for you. Just fill out this form please."

"How long will it take?" Ty asked.

"It's Friday. Won't be done over the weekend. It might be the middle of next week before we can give you the results."

"That's the soonest?" I asked disappointed.

"Could be ready by Tuesday, but I wouldn't count on it."

I finished filling out the form and left it with Lester's casket on the counter.

"We'll call you when it's ready," the receptionist said as we left.

Driving back to GH I asked Ty, "Do you think Ginger can tell that the grave has been disturbed?"

"Oh, I'm sure she can't. Whenever we get poor Lester back, we'll reinter him and all will be well. In the meantime, Ginger will never be any wiser. I just hope we don't spend big bucks only to find out Lester died of natural causes."

"If that's the case, I'll pay for the whole thing," I said, confident I was right. We'd agreed earlier to split the cost. Well, I was pretty confident.

CHAPTER THIRTEEN

The next day was Saturday and we'd agreed to return to Chapel Hill to track down some of Ralph's former neighbors. Unfortunately it was a rainy day which meant the top was up on the car. It didn't have quite the same panache as driving around with the top down.

Ty had printed out a Mapquest map to find the neighborhood which wasn't far from the University of North Carolina campus. It was a tree-lined street of older homes, a thoroughly appealing neighborhood. He pulled up in front of a house where the Duncans had lived before their move to Guilford City. It was a brick two-storey house probably built in the twenties or thirties. The yard was ablaze with deep pink and white azaleas.

"So what's the plan?" I asked.

"Let's talk to the neighbors on either side of their old house. Then we'll figure out where to go next."

He'd brought a big golf umbrella which we huddled under as we hurried up the front walk of the house on the right.

An elfin-like little old lady answered the doorbell.

"May I help you?" she asked.

"We're from Guilford City," I said, "and we've come here trying to find out some background on Ralph Duncan. We understand he lived next door."

"Why, yes, he and his wife did till they moved away a year or so ago. Why the questions?"

The rain started coming down in sheets and was bouncing off the slate porch unto my slacks. I introduced Ty and myself and asked "Could we come in for a minute? We won't take much of your time. We are trying to help out his wife Phyllis."

She seemed to realize we were on the verge of getting soaked and opened the door wide and beckoned us into the front hall. "If you don't mind," she said pointing at our wet shoes. We'd left the umbrella under the little overhang that sheltered the door, but it was true our shoes were wet and a little muddy. We obediently took them off and lined them up against the wall. Ty was wearing argyle socks, something I hadn't seen in years. They were kind of cute.

The woman, satisfied, led us into a living room that looked as if it hadn't changed since the nineteen-forties. Or maybe the twenties since the house probably had been built then. An upright piano held pride of place against the far wall next to a fireplace where a gas log burned in spite of the fact it was in the high sixties outside. The walls were painted deep green and the furniture, overstuffed and covered in flowery material, showed some wear but would qualify today as popular "shabby chic." Antimacassars protected the backs and arms of the chairs and sofa and were probably crocheted by our hostess. Floral hooked rugs covered the hardwood floors. I found the décor quite charming, and it seemed the perfect setting for its owner.

She perched on the edge of a painted Hitchcock chair that could have been handed down for generations from the look of it, its gold stenciling faded to a barely discernible representation of fruit across the back. She was cute as a button with fly-away white hair that framed her ruddy cheeks and her sparkling blue eyes. She wore a diminutive pantsuit which even then threatened to swallow her up. I wondered if she shopped in the children's department.

Ty and I sat on the sofa. "Your house is lovely," I said. "It reminds me of my childhood home in many ways."

Her name was Rosie McNamara, and, unsurprisingly, she had lived in the house all of her life. "I was an only child," she explained, "so there was no sibling rivalry over who would get this place. My father died rather young, and I took care of my mother when she developed Parkinson's. She died a quarter of a century ago. Now, enough about me. Where are you two from?"

"We live in a retirement center in Guilford City," I said, "but we both came here from out of state. I'm from upstate New York."

"And I recently lived in Maryland," Ty said. "I moved around quite a bit in my career."

"So, do you live in the place where the Duncans moved to? I knew they were going to some retirement home."

"Yes," Ty said. "In fact I live on the same hall at Glendon Hills."

"Glendon Hills? Is that the one that advertises it's for people in their 'golden years?' Who says old age is *golden*? What a crock!" Rosie's eyes were blazing as if she'd heard a slanderous statement she had to repudiate.

It was all I could do not to burst out laughing. This lady may have looked doll-like and benign, but she wasn't half as beatific as she appeared. She no doubt spoke her piece whenever the spirit moved her.

For a minute Ty seemed unable to come up with a reply. Finally he said, "Well, yes, as they say, 'old age isn't for sissies.' But I will say they try to make life as pleasant as possible."

"Well, I don't know about that. I just hope to die with my boots on, right here tending my roses or fixing my own dinner. I've lived here my whole life and I'm not about to move at this point in time."

I know a lot of people who feel the way Rosie does and more power to them. But I like the camaraderie of being with other folks and enjoy the perks that come with living at GH. To each his own I say.

"So why are you're asking about Ralph?" Rosie asked.

I wondered if Rosie was fond of him and this would come as a shock. But that didn't seem likely. "Ralph died week before last." I said.

She nodded her head. "Figures. Always thought he'd come to no good. Or was it natural?" So Rosie never expected him to succumb to anything normal like a heart attack.

"He was stabbed." Ty said.

She grimaced. "So what about poor Phyllis? How is she handling it? That poor woman went through hell with him."

"That's why we're here. Phyllis has been charged with killing Ralph."

"Oh, no," Rosie exclaimed. "She surely had reason enough to do it, but she was just too intimidated by him, lacking in self esteem. I can never in a million years imagine her doing such a thing. Now if it had been me..." She shrugged and gave a half grin.

It was almost comical to envision tiny little Rosie sticking a knife into 220-pound Ralph. But I was beginning to believe that nothing much would stop her once she made up her mind to do something.

"Do you think he physically abused her?" Ty asked.

"It's hard to tell exactly what goes on in someone else's house. But I think he pushed her around some. Don't think he beat her up and broke bones or anything. But he beat her down emotionally. Practically kept her prisoner. I tried to visit her or invite her over here for coffee but was never successful. The most we ever talked was across the fence in the back yard. She was kind of pathetic."

"What did she say?" I asked.

"Women like that are so ashamed they usually won't admit how bad their life is. I found out more from her friend Justine who lived on the other side of her than from Phyllis. I know Justine begged Phyllis to leave him, but she wouldn't do it."

"Justine is the one who convinced them to come to our place. I'm sure she thought Phyllis might be able to get out more and join in the activities," I said. "And Ralph wouldn't be able to have such a hold over her since we all live so close together."

"Did it work?"

"Unfortunately not," Ty said. "We rarely saw Phyllis. They never took meals in the dining room. Ralph, on the other hand, was more visible, but he didn't make any friends. People found him pretty off putting."

"Oh my, oh my. How very sad. I wish there was something I could do to help."

"We're operating under the theory that Phyllis did not do it."

"Amen to that," Rosie intoned.

"So we're looking at other possibilities. Did you ever hear or see anything that might indicate someone had a grudge against Ralph?" Ty asked.

A nearby clap of thunder made us all jump a little. If we had been acting in a play, I would say it heralded a great revelation. But life doesn't usually work that way.

Rosie thought a little and shook her head. "Off hand I can't think of anything."

Ty reached into his back pocket and pulled out his billfold. He opened it and pulled out a business card which he handed to her. "If you think of anything, please give me a call."

"What about the current neighbors on the other side of the Duncan's house? Could they tell us anything?" I asked.

"I very much doubt it. They moved in shortly before Ralph and Phyllis moved away. They're a young couple with kids so I don't think they had time to get acquainted. And the Duncan's weren't exactly the type to welcome the neighborhood newcomers."

We thanked Rosie, retrieved our shoes, and prepared to go back out in the rain. Ty went out the door first to put up the umbrella, and once I joined him, we ran down the front walk to the car getting pretty well soaked on the way.

Once in the car, Ty said, "I don't think there's much point in visiting anyone else on this street. Do you?"

"No. I'd like to get home and get dried out. By the way, I didn't know you still carried business cards."

He grinned as he put the key in the ignition. "Sure. It says 'Tyrone Landowski, Retiree Extraordinaire,' and gives my home phone and cell phone numbers. You never know when you might need one."

"Had you used one before?"

"No."

We were driving up Route 54 when I could hear a cell phone ringing.

"Is that yours?" I asked.

"Yeah," he said and pulled into a driveway. He reached into his jacket pocket and retrieved the phone.

"Yes?"

He didn't say anything else for quite a while. Finally he said, "Thanks," put the phone away and got back on the road.

"What was that about?"

"That was Rosie. She suddenly remembered a confrontation on the Duncan's front porch a couple of years ago. She said she was working in her garden and was behind some bushes where she couldn't be seen. She heard two men arguing and saw Ralph and a guy really going at it."

"Did she know who the other guy was?"

"She didn't recognize him, but she heard the name Farley. Said it stuck in her mind because it made her think of Farley Granger, the actor. She didn't know exactly what they were fighting about, but she heard Farley say, 'I'm gonna get you one of these days, Ralph. You better damn well watch your back.'"

"Oh ho," I said. "The plot thickens."

Maybe the thunder clap was prophetic after all. It was just a tad bit early.

CHAPTER FOURTEEN

Ty and I agreed not to involve ourselves in the case on Sunday. We needed a break, and it seemed appropriate to take Sunday off.

GH provides a Sunday brunch buffet but no supper is served that day. I'd said something the day before that my cupboards were bare because I hadn't had time to shop, and Ty confessed he was in the same boat. Because it was raining so hard on the way home from Chapel Hill we elected not to run into the grocery store, but agreed to get a light supper at a nearby Panera's Sunday night.

I piddled around paying bills, answering emails, and reading the Sunday paper, generally taking it easy all day. I met Ty in the lobby at 5:30 for the drive to Panera's. Luckily the rain had stopped the night before, and it was a pleasant evening.

Ty was unusually quiet on the way to the restaurant. I was curious as to what bothered him, but I knew he'd talk about it if and when he wanted to. He can be a very private person at times, and he doesn't appreciate anyone who tries to worm information out of him. He said very little until we had gone through the order line and were seated at a table with our bowls of soup. He rubbed his forehead for a while with his eyes closed, apparently pondering something of great significance.

"I don't know what to do, Vi. This decision is really getting me down."

"What decision?" It was obvious he was agonizing over something, but what?

"It's Perry. He calls me every day wanting to know if I'll get tested."

I'd gotten so wrapped up with Phyllis's predicament, Perry's request had temporarily slipped my mind. Ty hadn't mentioned it since Thursday so I guess I'd assumed the problem had simply gone away. Apparently not.

"Where is he?"

"He's staying in some motel around here. One of those you rent by the week I think."

"How's he getting his dialysis?"

"He can go to a local clinic. It looks like he's going to stay here and bug me until I make some kind of a decision."

"So what are you going to do?"

"I'd like to tell him to get lost. But it would probably haunt me if I did. Maybe I should go get tested. Surely the chances are slim that I would be a match. Then I can blow him off without it being on my conscience."

"And if it turns out you are a match?"

He just stared at me. I could tell he didn't want to go there. He took several sips of soup without answering. Finally he looked up. "Then I guess I'll decide fate has called on me, and I need to do what's best."

I reached over and patted his hand. "You're a good man, Ty. I know you want to do the right thing. On the other hand, you shouldn't feel like you're being railroaded in making such a big decision. Maybe it would help if you talked to his doctors about your feelings."

We didn't discuss it again that evening.

Monday morning when we met for coffee Ty told me he was going to see if he could track down Farley Lathrop. "It's a pretty unusual name so it shouldn't be too hard."

After exercise class Spunky came up to us. "Hi, guys. I'm dying of curiosity. Did it help to have the Duncan's old address in Chapel Hill?"

"We talked to one of her former neighbors. It just reinforced what we felt about Phyllis, that she wasn't capable of doing it," I said.

"Yeah," Ty said, "if we could only get concrete proof of that it would sure help."

"Well, keep trying. More power to you."

Ty and I went our separate ways. Ty was going online to see if he could find Farley while I went grocery shopping with lists for both of us. By doing his shopping for him I could at least free up some of his time for research. It was the first time I'd driven my seven-year old sedan in a while since we'd used Ty's car almost exclusively in recent days. Mine was pretty much of a bore compared to the little convertible, but I will say it had a lot more room to store multiple grocery bags.

I have a collapsible cart I use when I shop since it's a long walk from the parking lot to my apartment. After putting away my food, I took Ty's to him in the cart. His apartment is nicely furnished with expensive-looking leather furniture and tables made of glass and chrome. The accessories reflect his travels around the world and add pattern and color that make the room very appealing. It's surprisingly modern for an old codger like Ty.

"I've never asked, but did you have a designer for your apartment?"

"No, I did it myself. I've always liked good furniture."

"You have amazing taste, Ty."

"Well, thank you, Viola." He smiled. "One of my many hidden talents." He winked at me. I decided I had a lot to learn yet about Tyrone Landowski in spite of all the time we'd spent together.

"Made any progress?" I asked as I began to unload the bags onto his kitchen counter.

"I think I've tracked Farley down. He's in Burlington working at another car lot."

Burlington was about twenty-five miles northeast of Guilford City, closer than Chapel Hill.

"So are we going to go talk to him?"

"I think it might be a good idea. I'm sure he's not about to make a confession to us if, in fact, he did it. But at least we could size him up."

"Were you planning to go today?" It was already two-thirty in the afternoon.

"Tomorrow, if it works for you."

"Suits me." I'll latch on to any excuse to ride around in his little car.

"I've invited Perry to have supper with us tonight." Ty said as he put the milk and fruit away in the refrigerator.

That was a surprise. "Why? Have you made a decision?"

"I did some research on living donations. What I found is certain blood types are incompatible with others, and it's crucial to the surgery. So my thought was why even discuss going through testing if we found out before we started that our blood types were incompatible?"

"Are you saying if they are, you'd consider going ahead with it?"

"I've decided to take this one step at a time. I'll go where it leads me."

Ty is like that. Although he isn't particularly religious, I think he halfway believes in predestination. When the tides of life sweep him in a certain direction, he's willing to lie back and let them take him where they will.

We met Perry in the lobby at six that night. He was more obsequious than ever, practically licking Ty's boots in order to please him. But who could blame him? His life was at stake.

Ty was determined to keep the conversation light throughout the meal. He wasn't going to discuss anything relating to Perry's condition while we were in the dining room. I think he was afraid what Perry's reaction might be if they discovered they were not compatible by blood type.

Perry wasn't one for small talk, but he tried his best. I could tell that he wanted to cut out the chitchat and get down to the real reason for getting together. But in his anxiety he dropped his fork on the floor, knocked over a glass of water, and barely ate his food. The wait staff seemed agonizingly slow that evening which didn't help. But finally we finished the meal and headed up to Ty's apartment.

Ty and I sat on the sofa and Perry sat in a chair opposite us. His eyes were wide with anxiety, and I could see his hands shake a little. I felt terribly sorry for him.

"Perry, I want to discuss the guidelines for a transplant with you," Ty began. There was to be no beating around the bush now. "I read up on living donors on some websites, and I saw there were certain requirements as to the compatibility of blood types. It seems to me there is no sense in going any further with this unless we know whether or not we would be compatible. I'm assuming you know your blood type."

"Sure," Perry said.

"Well, I am AB," Ty said. "According to what I read that makes me a universal recipient but not a universal donor."

Perry's face lost all its color. He was crestfallen. "I'm blood type O." he said. "I can give to anyone, but my donor has to be an O as well. I don't know why I didn't think of that earlier. I'm just so frantic to find a match I put it out of my mind."

I thought he was going to cry. Well, at least Ty was off the hook. I was sure he was very grateful for that.

But I sat there mute. I have O positive blood.

Perry stood up. "Well, thank you, Tyrone, for at least checking it out. I know you meant well. Here's my card," He pulled a business card from his wallet and handed it to Ty. "Do keep in touch." He looked totally beaten down as if his last best hope was gone.

Ty walked him to the door but I stayed put. Ty came back to the living room and said, "Well, thank god that ordeal is over. At least Perry won't be bugging me any more."

I stood up. "I'm not feeling very well. I guess I'll go on home, Ty."

"What's wrong Vi?"

"I don't know. Maybe it was something I ate."

CHAPTER FIFTEEN

I didn't sleep well that night. Now I truly appreciated what Ty had been going through this past week. I wasn't going to share with Ty the knowledge of my compatibility. I knew the chances were probably slim that I would be a match in other ways, but I wondered if I should at least volunteer to be tested. I certainly had no obligation to do so, but still the thought haunted me.

I'd told him I wanted to do some laps in the pool before going to Burlington, so we decided to wait until after lunch to leave. I swam nearly twice as many as usual as a way to suppress the conflict that was warring in my mind. But it didn't do much good. My conscience was persistent in stealing into my thoughts no matter how hard I pushed myself trying to keep it out.

At lunch Ty commented that I seemed unusually quiet.

"Just tired I guess," I said. "I swam my butt off this morning. Needed the exercise." Not really, but it made a good excuse.

"Are you ready to hit the road?" He'd just polished off a piece of Kahlua chocolate cake that must have had 800 calories. Was it his way of celebrating the fact he wouldn't be giving a kidney? I had a bowl of raspberry Jello. This was a complete switch from our usual choices. Somehow it didn't make me feel virtuous.

It was another top-down day for the drive to Burlington.

The ride with the breeze in my face and my pink sparkly hat to hold down my hair did much to raise my spirits. It wasn't like we were going on a fun outing or that I expected a whole lot to come of the meeting with Farley, but riding through the beautiful countryside this time of year couldn't help but elevate my mood. Ty even started to sing "You are my Sunshine" in his beautiful baritone voice. I wished I could have joined in but my croaking would have totally spoiled it.

"Why don't you start a choral group of some kind at GH? You could call it the Golden Chorale like the Golden Corral, the restaurant," I said. "Maybe they could be your sponsor. Even if our friend Rosie hates the use of the word 'golden.'"

"Very funny," he said. "In fact I've thought about it a couple of times, but then I get involved with something else, like this investigation or whatever you want to call it, and I get sidetracked. Perhaps when this is all resolved I'll actually do something."

"You think it's going to get resolved?"

"You know what? I feel like I won't rest until we get Phyllis off the hook. In other words, by hook or by crook, we're going to find out who the real perpetrator is."

"I like your style, Ty Landowski. I'm with you all the way."

Alamance Pre-Owned Cars was on Church Street, the main east-west road through town. On the way we passed the city park that features a restored hundred-year-old carousel as the centerpiece.

"Some day I hope we can come and ride the merry-go-round," I said. "I've always wanted to do that."

"Don't you think your life is one already?" Ty asked.

"Well, since you put it that way, some days it seems like it. But, how about this? If we do find the perp who killed Ralph, I suggest we celebrate by coming over here for a ride."

He looked at me and grinned. "You're a funny sort, Viola. But if that turns you on, I'd be more than glad to join you for a spin on those horses."

"Deal?" I asked.

"Deal."

The car dealership was a lot less classy than the one where Farley had worked in Chapel Hill. To call the cars "pre-owned" was granting them a status higher than they deserved. It wasn't exactly Rent-A-Wreck, but it wasn't too many steps higher.

The salesman who watched us as we pulled in eyed Ty's car with relish. "Planning to trade it in?" he asked.

"Not today," Ty said, as if he might consider it next week. "I'm looking for Farley Lathrop. I understand he works here."

"He did until a couple of weeks ago. Then he got laid off. Car sales are slow, you know. Especially these gas guzzlers. The high price of gas has really put a dent in our business."

"Do you know where I can find him?"

"I can give you his address. You'd probably find him in his favorite bar though if he's not job hunting."

"I'd appreciate any help you can give me."

Ty followed the salesman inside to get the address while I stayed in the car. I studied all the nearby autos. Even though mine was seven years old, it looked better than anything I saw. In any case, I intend for the car and me to go out about the same time so I carefully nurse it along. It had only a little over fifty thousand miles and a lot of that was put on during my move to North Carolina. I hadn't done much driving since. A bus takes us to activities around the area, so all I need it for is the occasional run to the grocery store or other errands.

Ty came back shortly with Farley's home address and the address of a bar where he often hung out.

"Don't know how you feel about going in a bar," He said as he started the car. "This might not be in the best part of town."

"In that case I'd rather go in with you than sit in the car by myself."

We found the bar on a street I wouldn't want to be walking on alone. Mike's Tavern was a run-down looking place with windows across the front that might have once looked into a hardware store or small grocery. But they had been painted black so we had no clue what it might be like on the inside. Three tricked-out Harley's were parked along the curb. I was beginning to wonder if this was the dumbest thing we'd ever done, but I wasn't going to be the one to chicken out.

I know Ty wasn't happy about parking his car on this street, but since it was afternoon he probably hoped it would be safe in broad daylight.

"You sure you want to go in?" he asked as pulled up behind the cycles. "We can skip this place and go to his house."

"We're here so let's do it. We once had a guy come teach the Girl Scouts self defense, and he used me to demonstrate the moves. I know a little bit about kicking them in the shins and even more delicate places. So I'm good to go."

Ty laughed. "Just don't demonstrate any of the moves on me."

"I won't as long as you stay in line." Ty knew I was only kidding. He's a gentleman through and through.

It took a few minutes for my eyes to adjust to the darkness once we were inside. When I could finally make out the layout of the room, I saw that a long bar stretched across the entire back wall from one side to the other. The rest of the small space was taken up by a dozen or so small tables with deeply scarred tops and some ramshackle chairs. Since the windows had been painted over, the only light came from the neon beer signs that hung behind the bar and a couple of brass wall sconces on the side walls that gave out feeble rays. I wasn't sure if it was because they were very low wattage or the glass hadn't been washed in years.

Only a half dozen people were there. The three bikers perched on bar stools wore what seemed to be their "uniform:" jeans, sleeveless tee shirts that showed off their tattooed arms, and leather vests. Their Nazi-style helmets were lined up on the empty stools next to them. Surprisingly there was a couple as old as we are sitting at a table littered with beer bottles. An ashtray in the center of the table was piled high with cigarette butts, and they both were puffing away so hard that a haze had settled over the room. I was so used to living in a smoke-free environment that it was almost a shock to smell the pungent odor of cigarettes. I don't know if it was against the law to smoke in bars, but they obviously didn't care, and no one was preventing them from lighting up. The woman looked anachronistic in a wrinkled cotton housedress with socks and running shoes, and he wore bib overalls over a dingy shirt. One other man sat at the far left end of the bar twirling a glass on its surface and talking to the bartender. If anyone in the bar was Farley, it would have to be him.

I caught Ty's eye and tilted my head toward the man at the bar. He nodded agreement. As we walked up to stand next to him, he turned around to see who was approaching. A tall, gaunt man, he had curly black hair and a week's stubble on his chin. His eyes were bloodshot and looked glazed as if he already had a few drinks too many. He checked us out and turned back to his drink.

Ty sat down next to him and I sat on the other side of Ty.

"What can I get ya?" the bartender asked.

"How about a Corona," Ty said.

The bartender looked at me. "And you, Miss?"

"The same." I like an occasional beer even more than I like wine. My dad was a beer drinker—in moderation—and I'd developed a taste for it when he deemed I was old enough to drink, which in his mind was eighteen. He didn't care what the law said if I only drank it at home. When I went to college, there were always beer parties, but the drinking never got to the extreme it has these days where the kids swill beer through hoses till they pass out. I'm not so sure I could handle the social scene at college the way it is today. There are times when I'm glad I come from a different generation.

The barkeep slapped two foaming mugs down in front of us. Then Ty turned to the man next to him who was drinking some kind of mixed drink and asked, "Farley?"

The man almost dropped his glass and stared at Ty in surprise.

"Do I know you?" he asked. He had a faint slur to his speech.

"No. But I'd like to talk to you about an acquaintance of yours."

"Who's that?" Farley asked suspiciously.

"Could we move to that table over there so we can speak in confidence?" Ty said pointing to a table on the opposite side of the room from the couple. They seemed so absorbed in each other and their cigarettes I doubted they'd be interested in anything we had to say anyway.

"S'pose so," Farley said as he rose from his stool and had to steady himself by hanging onto the bar to keep from falling back onto the seat. I wasn't sure he was in any shape to interrogate, but since we'd been lucky enough to find him, Ty probably thought he should get what he could out of him.

Ty took hold of his arm and half supported, half steered Farley to the table he'd indicated. Farley fell into the chair Ty pulled out for him.

"My drink!" Farley cried, pointing back toward the bar. "I need my drink."

I'd brought the two beers with me but had my hands full. "I'll get it," I said. I knew we'd get nothing from him unless we helped lubricate his tongue enough to get it wagging. I asked the bartender to top it off before I took it to Farley. Did I feel guilty about it? Not really. All's fair in war, and I considered this a war.

Farley drank from it gratefully. "So who are you and how'd you know my name?"

"I'm Ty and she's Vi. Easy to remember because it rhymes. We know who you are because we talked to George Grant."

Farley smiled. "Oh, yeah, Georgie Porgy. Good guy. Sorry I left his place."

"Why did you, Farley?" Ty asked.

"Thought I could do better. Would you believe I got a job with a builder? God, I was making good money for a while. But after a few months the bottom dropped out and pretty soon I wasn't making squat. I was let go."

"Did you try to get your old job back?" I asked.

"Yeah. But George's business was down too. Said he was sorry but he couldn't use me."

"But Alamance Pre-Owned Cars could," Ty prompted.

Farley took a big gulp of his drink. "At first they were doin' okay 'cause people wanted to buy cheap cars. Then gas prices started to go up, and they no longer wanted gas guzzlers. So I was out on the street again. This damn recession or whatever you want to call it is the pits. The only thing I could find was in a fast food joint. Damned night shift too. It sucks." He looked like he was about to cry.

I felt for him and all the other men and women who were having such a tough time these days. I was thankful I was no longer at an age where I needed a job to support myself. I knew even the Girl Scouts were struggling along with everyone else. They were consolidating councils, and I could have ended out on the street like this poor man.

Farley seemed to withdraw into himself, nursing his wounded ego.

"We wanted to ask you about Ralph Duncan," I said, deciding we should get to the point before Farley went into a complete funk.

It was as if I said the magic words.

Farley's head came up and he hissed, "That SOB."

"Why is that?" I asked.

Farley rolled his eyes. "The guy's a cheater. He cheats ever'body."

"How'd he do that?" Ty asked. Ty was talking to him like a psychologist would talk to a patient: non-confrontational, soothing, acting as if what Farley had to say was the most important thing in the world. He could sweet talk almost anything out of anybody. Wish I had such a silver tongue.

"He cheated me 'n' George out of commissions," he said as he thumped the table with his fist. "An' he cheated on his wife too."

CHAPTER SIXTEEN

Ty and I looked at each other. A new revelation. Was this going to work against Phyllis? It seemed like another motive the prosecution could throw out on the table.

"How do you know that, Farley?" I asked

"Ever'body knew it. He weren't too subtle about it. Liked to brag 'bout his 'conquests,' dirty bastard."

"We heard you and he got into a fist fight one day at work. And then a neighbor of Ralph's heard you threaten him at his house. What was that about?" Ty asked.

He waved a dismissive hand. "I don' remember exactly. The guy just got to me so bad I prob'ly blew up. He had a way of gettin' under your skin. Besides I was prob'ly drunk."

He took another long swallow of his drink, emptying the glass. "Are you gonna get me another?" he said waving the glass in the air. "What's all these questions about anyways?"

It went against the grain but I got up. "I'll refill it if you promise not to drive, Farley."

"Can't drive. Lost my car along with ever'thing else. I live in a room a couple of blocks from here. Only place I can afford."

I got him another drink and hoped he didn't pass out before we were through questioning him.

He took another swallow and said, "So what's this all about?"

"Ralph Duncan is dead," I told him.

His eyes got wide. "No joke! Well, the earth's a better place now. Wha' happened to him?"

"He was stabbed," Ty said. "The Duncans were in a retirement center in Guilford City. Same place we live."

"Did his wife do it? The way he cheated on her wouldn't surprise me."

"Unfortunately the cops think so. We don't happen to agree with them," I said.

"I didn't know the lady. She never came 'round."

"I understood she came to the dealership to plead with George to keep Ralph on after he fired him. You didn't see her then?" Ty asked.

"Must of been my day off. I remember George telling me about it. Said he felt real sorry for her. But he couldn't put up with Ralph no more."

"Let's say we're right and Phyllis didn't do it. Can you think of anyone who might?" I asked

Farley looked into his glass like he was studying tea leaves hoping for an answer. Finally he quit staring and gulped down the rest of the drink. He was swaying now, and I didn't think he was going to be able to answer any more questions.

"Don' know," he said tilting his glass from side to side and staring at it again as if he were hoping more liquid would magically appear. "I think ever'one he ever knew hated his guts so much it could be anybody." He put down the glass, crossed his arms on the table, laid his head down, and either fell asleep or passed out.

I looked at Ty and shrugged. He stood up and went to the bar and slapped down a bill to cover the drinks. Then he took my arm and we left. The bikers were still drinking, and the smokers were still smoking, and none of them paid any attention to us.

"Well, that wasn't too productive," I said. "Everyone says pretty much the same thing about Ralph."

"Nobody told us he cheated on Phyllis before," Ty said as he started the car which remained unsullied, much to his relief. "That isn't exactly going to help her if it gets out."

"Oh, I'm sure the cops will find out about it. You notice that no one has said the police have already talked to them?"

"Maybe they haven't gotten around to it yet. The prosecution probably will have an investigator making his rounds questioning people eventually."

"I guess when they're so sure they've charged the right person, they take their time doing the background checks," I said. "If any of these people we've interviewed tells them we'd been asking questions about Ralph, there might be hell to pay for interfering in their case."

Ty scowled. "Hadn't thought of that. Though I don't see how they could stop us. Free speech and all that. But maybe, just for the sake of covering our asses, I should call them and ask them not to mention we'd been talking to them. What do you think?"

"Can't hurt."

Ty had programmed each person's phone number into his cell phone as he interviewed them, so he pulled out his phone and called each of them on the spot. Everyone agreed not to mention we'd been there unless they were asked directly about us in which case they couldn't lie. I doubted very much the investigator would think to do that. Farley was in a stupor back inside the bar so we decided to let that go. He'd probably forgotten our conversation anyway.

"The one person we haven't talked to is Ed Stillman," Ty said as he pulled away from the curb.

The name didn't ring a bell. "Who's that?"

"Ray Fantana at Fantana Fencing gave us his name. He was the one Ralph cheated out of commissions."

"That seemed to be his favorite pastime," I said. "He must have cheated people right and left."

"To say nothing of cheating on Phyllis."

"Yeah, there's that too."

"I haven't been able to track Ed down yet," Ty said. "But I'll keep trying. I can't say I have any strong feelings at this point that anyone we've talked to could be the perp. How do you feel?"

"I agree with you. What little we've found out seems to hurt Phyllis rather than help her."

"I know," Ty said. "Pretty discouraging."

We were back at GH in time for dinner. I went to my apartment first to freshen up and planned to meet Ty in the dining room. I checked my phone to see if I had any messages and the beep-beep indicated I did.

It was the emergency vet's office telling me that the autopsy report was in on Ginger's bird. I'd been so caught up in our interviews I'd forgotten they'd said it would probably be back today. I was glad the clinic was open at night so we could get the results that evening.

When I told Ty about the message over dinner he couldn't wait to go there. He always polished off his meal much faster than I did, and tonight was no exception.

"Come on, Vi. Eat your veggies and finish your salad. You're a pokey eater."

"Darn it, Ty. I hate being rushed. It gets my digestion all out of sorts. Maybe you ought to go eat with the Bridge Dudes from now on instead of me. They always scarf it down so they can get back to the bridge table."

He looked repentant. "I'm sorry. Some days I think my patience quotient is shrinking every day I get older."

"Well, just relax and let me eat at my own pace. The place is open till midnight."

And so he folded his hands and settled back in his chair and tried very hard to appear mellow. However, I spied his foot tapping impatiently under the table. That only tempted me to slow down even more. Some days I don't know why he wants to put up with me. Other days it is vice versa.

We finally left for the vet clinic after I took my time eating peach cobbler. I've often thought our relationship must be like young brothers and sisters who feel compelled to needle and torment each other. Since I was an only child and didn't have that experience early in life, I figured I might as well enjoy it now.

We went into the clinic together, anxious to learn what the report said.

"Can we talk to the doctor about it?" I asked the receptionist. I wanted to make sure we didn't misinterpret the findings.

"Sure, if you don't mind waiting fifteen or twenty minutes or so. He's with somebody at the moment."

We agreed and settled into the uncomfortable plastic chairs in the waiting area. As always, the magazines on the side tables were months old and mostly geared toward men, the main topic being cars or sports. Of course Ty snatched up one glorifying cars and became engrossed in it. I was glad something had sidetracked his impatience over the autopsy results.

It was forty-five minutes later when the vet came out and asked us to follow him to his office. Dr. Rostov was a young man with blond hair and a kind face. In fact, when he smiled, it was almost beatific. If I hadn't already had a vet for Sweetie, I would have considered bringing her here. She, like many cats, was not a happy camper when I had to put her in the carrier to take her in for a check up. Dr. Rostov looked like he could qualify to be a cat or dog "whisperer" and calm them down.

"Okay," he said as we settled in chairs across the desk from him. "The necropsy shows that the bird died of a broken neck," he said, reading from the report. "The bones had been crushed." His smile was long gone. I could tell it hurt him to learn that any kind of animal or bird was mistreated.

He pulled out an x-ray and pointed out the region to us where the small vertebrae were visibly damaged. "We opened him up as well as taking the pictures. Wanted to see exactly how much damage was done."

"Could this have conceivably happened in an accident?" I asked.

"Not unless the bird was loose and some animal got hold of it. But I'd be much more likely to believe it was done by human hands."

"Its owner found him dead on the floor of the cage, so it couldn't have gotten out," Ty said.

"Any chance the owner was responsible, but refused to admit it?" Dr. Rostov asked.

"Oh, my gosh, no," I said. "She loved that bird so much. She was devastated when she found him dead."

"Are you going to let her know our findings?" he asked.

"Not if I can help it. She's having a hard time getting over it. That would make it so much worse for her. To think someone deliberately killed him."

We thanked him, picked up the makeshift casket with Lester's remains and headed back to GH.

"Are we going to put this back in the ground tonight?" Ty asked on the way.

"I think we should. It's almost dark. I'll go get my trowel and meet you out back of the building."

As soon as we got home, I gathered up my trowel and miniature light from the apartment and met Ty out at the edge of the woods. It took us no time to find and dig up the plot again. There was a new bouquet of flowers on top so we knew Ginger had been out there. But she must have been none the wiser that the burial plot was temporarily empty. Had she known, I'm sure the whole building would be aware of it by now.

We quickly reinterred the casket and placed the bouquet back on top.

"By the way," I said. "I owe you for part of the autopsy. Remember I said I'd pay for the whole thing if I was wrong? Since I was right I only owe you half."

"Forget it. I was sure you'd be right. Never doubted it. Since you came up with that great idea, I'll pay for all of it. It's the least I can do."

CHAPTER SEVENTEEN

We both had no doubt someone with a pass key to the apartments killed Lester. And of course it seemed reasonable that same person was the perp who killed Ralph. It was the only scenario that made sense, I thought, provided you didn't believe Phyllis was guilty. It was one small step closer to solving the crime (at least from our point of view), but there was still a long way to go.

I asked Ty when we had coffee together if he thought we ought to tell Cliff about our findings.

"Good idea," he said. "It might make a difference on how he plans to defend her. And maybe he has investigators who can track down people better than we can."

After exercise class I called Greta.

"Ty and I discovered something interesting that Cliff should know about. Could you guys come to dinner one night so we can discuss it?" I asked.

"Wouldn't you rather come over here and have a break from your dining room?"

We have very good food in our dining room, but sometimes it seems a bit repetitious so I always jump at the chance to eat somewhere else. I think Ty feels the same way.

"Well, sure. I never turn down a chance to eat out. Especially your cooking," I added as Greta truly was an exceptional cook. And I knew she loved to entertain, so I didn't feel guilty about it.

"How about tomorrow night then?"

Ty had already told me his evenings were free for the rest of the week so I accepted her invitation.

Ty had said he was going to play bridge that afternoon, and I rather felt at loose ends. I realized I hadn't checked on Phyllis in almost a week and felt bad about it even though I had spent most of the time working for her vindication. I called her after lunch and asked her if she was up to having company.

Phyllis sounded more depressed than before which alarmed me. It was as though she could barely summon the strength to speak.

When I went to her apartment she greeted me in a robe and pajamas. She looked unkempt with uncombed hair and no makeup, and almost disoriented in her jerky movements.

She apologized that she had nothing to offer me. "I don't make coffee any more because I can't sleep as it is, and I don't need caffeine to make it worse," she said. Lack of sleep was revealed by the bruised-looking pouches below her eyes and the fatigue she displayed in her every move. I felt even worse now that I hadn't visited her sooner.

"I'm so sorry," I said, embarrassed by how totally inadequate that sounded. But what can you say? "Has your doctor prescribed sleeping pills?"

That brought on tears. Lots of tears.

Finally she wiped her cheeks with the sleeve of her robe. "Oh, god, Viola, I think that's what got me into trouble in the first place."

"What do you mean?" I was alarmed now. Something must have come up that I didn't know about.

"I'd been taking those new sleeping pills that are supposed to work so well. And before Ralph died, I found out I'd been going to the kitchen in my sleep and getting something to eat. It was so weird. I'd discover the crusts of sandwiches and dirty drinking glasses on the counter in the morning. It worried me, but I was so desperate for sleep I kept on taking the medicine."

"Oh my gosh, Phyllis. That's scary. I've even heard of people driving cars when they were under the influence of those pills."

She broke down into sobs, and I sat beside her on the couch and put my arm around her shoulder to comfort her. Something about those pills was weighing heavily on her.

When she got herself under control she said, "The more I think about it, the more I wonder if I actually *did* kill Ralph in my sleep. My head is so muddled any more I can't be sure what happened. I'll never take another sleeping pill in my life!"

Was that possible? It certainly didn't seem likely, but if she was going to waver in her conviction that she was innocent, what was that going to do for her case? Was this something that Cliff should know? I decided *I* wasn't going to tell him. He'd probably learn about it from Phyllis eventually, but not from me. But it seemed the harder we worked to exonerate her, the more things seemed to coalesce against her.

"Oh, Phyllis," I said as I hugged her, "I doubt very much that is true. Remember you told us how you found him on the living room floor with the knife beside him?"

"I know," she sniffed. "But now it all seems like some strange nightmare, and I don't know any more what I saw or what I did. Maybe that was all part of a dream I was having, and I only *thought* it was true. Or maybe I killed him in my sleep and then woke up to find him on the floor."

"Have you thought of asking your doctor for some tranquilizers?"

She shook her head vigorously. "I don't want to feel doped up. I'm enough of a mess already."

"Sometimes we need a little help to get over the biggest humps." I wanted desperately to suggest something that would help her, but I couldn't seem to come up with any solutions she would accept.

She put her elbows on her knees and cradled her head in the palms of her hands as she stared at the floor. She had nothing more to say. I was truly alarmed at her condition. I sat for a few more minutes, but she didn't move or speak, so I got up and said, "I'll be going now, Phyllis, but please let me know if there's anything I can do for you." I'd never felt so useless in my life.

She gave no response so I let myself out. I hurried home and called Babs Osborne who had counseled Phyllis right after Ralph died. Perhaps she could convince her to seek help. She was going to fall to pieces if she didn't get it soon. Babs readily agreed to go see her.

"I'll do my best," she said. "But Phyllis has such an ingrained sense of self loathing she's awfully hard to reach. She needs regular appointments with a psychologist to work out all of her many problems, but I couldn't convince her earlier to do it, and I doubt I can convince her now."

"Well, thanks for trying," I said. "I guess that's all any of us can do till Phyllis makes up her mind to seek help."

Phyllis's entrenched refusal to ask for assistance reminded me that she was the opposite of Perry's overbearing attempts to get support for a kidney transplant. If only she had a smidgen of his drive and stubbornness. But thinking of Perry brought on disturbing thoughts that I wanted to ward off the way Phyllis rejected us. I knew I could possibly be a kidney donor if I had the will to be tested, but I kept pushing that thought back into the inner recesses of my mind so it wouldn't taunt me. Sometimes it wouldn't always stay there, and when that happened I had some sleepless nights as well.

When I returned to my apartment after swimming laps in the pool Thursday morning I had a message on my phone from Ty.

"Since we're at a standstill as far as Phyllis is concerned, I'm going to run some errands this afternoon. I'll meet you in the lobby at 5:30 to go to your niece's.

I decided I needed some catch-up time as well. I started out with the intent of going through my summer clothes that had been stored away and see what I could wear since warm weather was imminent. Unfortunately the good food here had added pounds, and I was afraid that none of my clothes would fit any more. It annoyed me no end how the weight had snuck up on me, but I wasn't quite ready to refuse the desserts that were offered in the dining room. The vegetables they served might not always be to my liking, but I never met a dessert I didn't love.

After about fifteen minutes of trying on too small tops and slacks I felt so demoralized I decided to spend the rest of the afternoon reading. That's always a good way to fend off one's troubles for a little while anyway. Immerse yourself in a good story.

Ty and I met at the appointed hour and drove to the Holcomb residence. On the way I filled him in on my visit with Phyllis.

"You mean she really thinks she might have killed him while under the influence of a sleeping pill?" Ty sounded incredulous.

"That's what she says. I've never heard of such a thing, but I do know people have done strange things after taking them. I'm not sure I convinced her that it didn't happen that way."

"Oh, man, that's not good. It means she's not going to insist on her innocence," Ty said. "Do you suppose we could talk to a doctor and find out if it would even be possible?"

"That's not a bad idea, Ty. But, in the meantime, I don't want to be the one that tells Cliff about this. He'll probably hear it from her eventually, but I don't want to be the bearer of more bad news."

"I agree. Let's just stick with the Lester incident. Stick with the positive."

I couldn't help but be a little nervous about how Cliff would respond to the information we were going to share with him. He might be pleased at what we'd discovered or he might be angry at us for interfering in his case. If it was the latter, I don't know whether we'd be too discouraged to continue our investigation or feel empowered to carry on.

CHAPTER EIGHTEEN

We were ushered into the Holcomb's beautiful living room where a fire burned merrily in the fireplace once more adding that special ambience of hospitality. Cliff greeted us with a smile and handshake. He always was the epitome of a gracious host.

As usual they served a round of drinks, wine for Greta and me, whiskey sour for Ty, and Vodka martini for Cliff. They didn't have to ask because we always requested the same thing. This was the time for small talk and conviviality so we steered away from any talk concerning Phyllis.

Greta had prepared a wonderful meal of beef filet, garlic mashed potatoes and asparagus. She knew that asparagus was perhaps my very favorite vegetable and often served it when she invited me to dinner. And even Ty couldn't resist her home made peach cobbler.

It wasn't till the dessert was served that I brought up the topic we wanted to discuss. I was pretty nervous about how Cliff would respond.

I tried to put it in the best possible light. "You know, Cliff, something strange happened the morning that Ralph Duncan was killed."

He was so busy enjoying the cobbler I wasn't sure if he heard me or not.

"That so?" he said with his mouth half full.

But I powered on. "One of their neighbors had a pet parrot. Ty ran into her in the hall, and she was quite distraught because she found her parrot dead."

Cliff finally looked up from his dessert. "I hate those birds. Why on earth would anyone want to keep one is beyond me. Jabber, jabber."

"Well, she was very attached to this one. The funny thing is the bird had picked up some X-rated language from her late husband and repeated it all the time. It was embarrassing to visit her while Lester was spewing expletives." This wasn't germane to what I wanted to tell him but I thought the humor of it might soften him up a little.

Cliff had a hearty laugh over that. "That's rich. One way to keep visitors away if you'd rather be alone, I guess."

"I think she's a little obtuse," Ty said. "She loved him because he reminded her of her husband. I don't think it entered her mind that others would find it offensive. I wonder if the gal is sliding into dementia."

"I hadn't thought of that," I said.

"So? I'm sure you have a point here," Cliff said. Now that he had finished his dessert he gave us his full attention.

"Mainly she was distraught because he was twenty-five years old. She said they can easily live to be fifty or so. Anyway she put the bird in a metal box and buried it out in the woods behind our building. She puts fresh flowers on top of the grave. That's how much she cared."

Cliff had a look of amusement on his face as if we'd lost it over some bird. He shrugged and said, "And?"

"Vi and I got to thinking that it was strange a healthy bird would die so suddenly," Ty said. "We wondered if someone helped it along."

"So we came up with a hypothetical scenario," I took over the story. "What if someone had a master key to all the apartments? He let himself into Ginger's by mistake thinking it was the Duncan's. The bird woke up and started to make sounds. So he opened the cage door and strangled it so it wouldn't alert its owner."

"Realizing he made a mistake, he then left and went to the Duncan's apartment and killed Ralph which was his aim in the first place," Ty continued.

"Sounds pretty far fetched to me," Cliff said.

"What if I told you we dug up the bird and got a necropsy on it?" I watched the expression on his face. It changed from befuddlement to wariness.

"Do you guys think you're Monk or something?" he said referring to the TV show. Perhaps we did seem as off-the-wall as that character.

I chose not to answer that question. "The bird died of a broken neck," I said. "And I'm darn sure its owner didn't do it."

"Look, you just said she might be slipping into dementia," Cliff pointed out.

I was angry now. "Darn it, Cliff. That doesn't mean she'd kill her beloved bird. Lester meant everything to her."

Cliff wiped his mouth with his napkin and laid it on the table. "That sounds just a bit too far fetched you guys. How about leaving the investigation to me and my staff? I know you mean well, but you're just muddying the waters."

Greta had been sitting silently listening to all the back and forth. "It makes sense to me, Cliff. Why won't you at least consider the possibility of it happening that way?" I wanted to kiss her.

He gave her a rather patronizing smile. "Now, Greta, you've never questioned how I've handled cases before. Please don't start now."

She frowned. "You've never discussed them with me so how could I?"

"That's the whole point. I don't think we should be discussing this one either."

I loved Cliff. He'd always been so good to me. But I was furious with him now. He was acting as if we hardly had good sense. I bit my lip so I wouldn't say anything I'd regret, but finally I couldn't contain myself "Okay, I get what you're saying. We should butt out." Well, maybe that was stronger than I meant it to be but, I couldn't help it.

Cliff laughed. "I wouldn't put it that crudely, Vi. Let's just say I think I have things under control. *If* I find I need your help, I'll let you know."

Yeah, how likely would that be?

We spent the rest of the evening in small talk, but I was so disappointed I could barely join in. I could tell Greta sensed that and kept trying to pull me into the conversation, but I couldn't conquer my disappointment at Cliff's response. He could at least have said he'd give it some thought and then forgotten about it. At least that wouldn't have seemed so disparaging.

Finally we said we should be getting back and said our farewells. Greta gave me an extra long hug, and I knew she sympathized with us. But there was little she could do about it.

On the way back home Ty said, "Well, that went over like a lead balloon. Are we wasting our time, Vi? If he's not going to listen to us what's the point?"

"The point is I think we're on to something. And I, for one, am not going to let Cliff discourage me from checking out what we can. Are you thinking of bailing out?"

He turned and grinned at me. "Atta girl. I was hoping you'd say that. I'm sticking with you, kid."

CHAPTER NINETEEN

After exercise class on Friday I suggested to Ty that we visit Phyllis. I'd been alarmed at her state of mind the day before and thought it would be prudent to check on her. We took the elevator up to the fourth floor of the East Wing and knocked on her door. Only silence followed. We knocked again and called out her name, but there was no response.

"I don't like this," I said. "Phyllis very rarely leaves her apartment. I'm worried something is wrong."

Ty reached for the door handle, we have handles rather than knobs because they're easier for arthritic hands, and tried it. It wasn't locked.

"Do you think we should go in?" he asked.

"I do. Why don't you let me go in first in case she's not dressed," I said.

He waited in the hall while I proceeded slowly into the apartment calling her name. The kitchen was empty as was the living room. I went down the hall toward her bedroom and found the bedroom door closed. I knocked on it and called her name again. No answer. Finally I opened the door slowly and looked in. If she was asleep I didn't want to disturb her.

The room was quite dark. She had a room darkening shade on the window that was very effective, and it took a couple of minutes for my eyes to adjust to the gloom. Finally I could see well enough to make out a form on the bed. I was surprised she was still asleep so late in the morning, but thought she'd probably been up very late the night before. She'd said she'd been fighting insomnia, and perhaps she hadn't been able to doze off until early morning.

I decided not to disturb her and was about to leave when I noticed some dark stains on the blanket that covered her. My eyes had finally adjusted to the dim light well enough I could now make them out. I walked over to her, and realized it was blood. I pulled the blanket back and found her arms crossed over her chest. Both wrists had long cuts that were oozing blood which had soaked through the blanket.

I'd been worried about her state of mind, but it hadn't occurred to me that she would resort to this. I shook her shoulder to see if she was conscious. She moaned but didn't open her eyes. I picked up the phone on the bedside table and dialed 911 and explained the circumstances to the operator. After I hung up I pushed on the emergency call button that alerted the staff downstairs. I knew they would send someone immediately.

Then I hurried back to Ty who was standing in the hall waiting for me.

"She tried to kill herself," I told him. "She slashed her wrists though the cuts don't seem to be too deep. I've called 911 and alerted them downstairs."

"Oh god," he said. "Poor woman. I feel so sorry for her."

"Why don't you wait here for the EMTs, and I'll go stay with her," I said.

I went back to the bedroom and raised the shade and light flooded the room. I noticed how pale she looked but didn't think she'd bled enough to threaten her life. Then I glanced into the attached bathroom and saw that the sink was splattered with dark red. She must have cut her wrists there before climbing into bed and pulling up the blanket. Maybe she'd lost more blood than I realized. I went into the bathroom, pulled two hand towels off the towel bar and wrapped one around each wrist to try and stop the flow. I was perched on the side of the bed holding the towels in place when Brad, our daytime security man, came rushing into the room. I knew he had some emergency training so I let him take over. Phyllis seemed to have slipped deeper into unconsciousness as she didn't react when he spoke to her.

"What happened?" he asked as he examined her wrists.

"I don't know exactly. I've been worried about her so we came to visit. When she didn't answer the door it alarmed us, so I tried it and it was unlocked. I came in and found her like this."

"Did you call 911?" he asked.

"I called them first. They should be here soon."

He had brought a small first aid kit with him and proceeded to wrap her wrists with gauze. He was checking her vital signs when the EMTs appeared.

They shooed us out of the room so we went out into the hall where a gurney waited. Some of the neighbors were now coming out to find out what the commotion was all about.

Ginger was one of the first to appear.

"Has something happened to Phyllis?" she asked.

"She's not well," I told her. It certainly wasn't the whole truth, but I didn't want to start tongues wagging about her again. There'd been enough talk about her after Ralph's death, and I didn't want to add any fuel to the fire.

"I'm beginning to wonder if this hall is jinxed or something," Ginger said. "Bad things keep happening here. It worries me."

I wanted to reassure her, but I didn't know what to say. "It's just a coincidence that several things have happened on this particular hall recently. We're all vulnerable to health problems at our age."

She harrumphed and shook her finger at me. "You call murder a *health problem*?"

Well, I guess she had a point. I felt foolish. "No, of course not. Didn't mean to be flip about it."

"And my dear Lester wasn't a *health problem* either. I still don't understand that at all."

I hoped she never would. "That was sad," I agreed, and then decided to keep my mouth shut before I said anything else I'd regret.

Ty and I decided there was nothing else we could do there, and we were all pretty much in the way. "Let's leave it to the EMTs," Ty said, "and the rest of us go home."

The neighbors began to return to their apartments, and Ty and I decided we should visit Justine and fill her in on Phyllis.

We went to the second floor and knocked on her door.

"What a nice surprise," she said when she opened it.

"Not so nice I'm afraid," I said as we stepped into her apartment. "We just came from Phyllis's, and she's on her way to the hospital."

"Oh, no. What happened?"

"I found her with her wrists cut."

Justine's eyes began to tear up. "I knew she was depressed. I never thought she'd do anything like that. Oh, poor Phyllis. How bad is it?"

"I think she lost a lot of blood. But I don't think it's life threatening."

Justine started looking frantically around the room. "I've got to go to the hospital to be with her. If only I could remember where I left my purse."

Ty was standing in the hall next to the kitchen. "It's here on the kitchen table," he said. Everyone here has their senior moments. It's normally a matter for levity but not so much in this case.

She walked over and grabbed it, opened the coat closet door and pulled out a light jacket. "If you'll excuse me, I'm in a hurry."

"I'm glad you're going," Ty said. "She'll really need someone to be there for her. Let us know if there's anything we can do."

As we left Justine's and headed downstairs again I said to Ty, "This means it's even more urgent to find out what happened to Ralph.

Apparently Phyllis has convinced herself she did it under the influence of sleeping pills, and she's lost her will to live."

"I think you're right. The one name we have that we haven't been able to contact is Ed Stillman, Ralph's coworker at the fencing company. I can't seem to get a lead on him."

"What if we go back over to the fencing company and talk to Ray Fantana again. He would probably know who some of his friends or acquaintances are. Maybe we could run him down that way."

"Well, it's worth a try anyway. It beats sitting around and twiddling our thumbs. It's close to lunchtime. Want to eat here or catch something on the way?"

"Let's eat in Chapel Hill."

"Sounds like a plan."

It was a perfect day to be riding in Ty's convertible. The sky was clear, the temperature was in the high sixties, and something about that car made me feel young again, even if I almost needed a lift to get me out of the low-slung seat. My sequined cap kept my hair out of my eyes, and I hummed quietly along with Ty as he sang songs popular in the fifties. It's amazing how you never forget the words to the songs you loved when you were young. I couldn't begin to recite the words to any song written in the past two or three decades.

We found a little sandwich shop in downtown Chapel Hill and had our lunch. Surrounded by college kids, we reminisced about our own college days. Ty had gone to Brown where he majored in Political Science, and I went to Ohio State and majored in extracurricular activities. Technically I was an English major but my interests and the bulk of my time were devoted to groups like the YWCA and the campus newspaper. That was back in the day when resident fees were dirt cheap, and I lived at home and commuted by city bus, so it wasn't necessary to have a part time job to pay the bills. On the other hand Ty's education as an out-of-state student at a private university was much more expensive, and he worked at a number of odd jobs throughout his student days. The sandwich shop where we ate reminded him of his job at a deli near campus.

"I put on fifteen or twenty pounds when I worked there," Ty said while we waited for our order. "I got freebies and I kind of went overboard."

"I can't imagine you ever being overweight," I said.

"I wasn't really fat, but I got a bit of a paunch. It alarmed me so much I quit and found another job working in a drugstore. Not nearly as much fun, but I did manage to lose the extra weight. That's why I eat so carefully now. Don't want to put on pounds. They're too hard to get off."

"You know what, Ty?" I said. "I figure life is too short, and at my age I'm going to take my pleasure where I can find it. I'm not about to give up a piece of chocolate cake because I'm worried about my waistline."

"More power to you, my dear. You always look good to me. I don't subscribe to the notion you can never be too thin. Ladies who believe that look like concentration camp survivors."

I thought it was gallant of him to say that but was not convinced he really meant it. But that was Ty. Always the gentleman.

The waitress arrived with our meals. I had to laugh because I had ordered a Reuben sandwich with potato salad while Ty had a garden salad with fat-free dressing. At least I hadn't ordered dessert this time.

After lunch we drove to Fantana Fencing to speak to Ray Fantana.

When we walked in the door he was behind the counter. He looked at us as if he thought he knew who we were but couldn't quite place us.

Ty put out his hand for a shake. "Remember us, Ray? We were here a week or so ago to talk to you about Ralph Duncan."

"Oh, right," Ray said shaking Ty's hand. "How are you doing? Have you run down the perp?"

"'Fraid not. That's why we're back. We'd like to track down Ed Stillman if possible."

"Like I said, I don't know what happened to him."

"We know that," I said. "But we thought maybe you might know who he hangs out with or where he hangs out. Anything at all you can tell us to help us find him."

Ray pursed his lips as he thought about that. "I remember he belonged to a motorcycle club."

"You mean like Hell's Angels?" I asked. I wasn't so sure I wanted to track down a guy who belonged to that.

"No. It's a group made up of mostly middle-aged men. Some of them are professionals like lawyers and CPAs and the like. But there are some like Ed too. Guys who don't have highfaluting jobs but love to ride. Sometimes they do charity rides; sometimes they just like to take off for the Parkway or somewhere like that."

The Blue Ridge Parkway has always attracted motorcycle riders. Its gorgeous scenery and 45-mile-per-hour speed limit make it a relatively safe place for them. It was within two or three hours' ride from here.

"So where do they hang out?" Ty asked.

"There's a motorcycle shop on the east side of town. Bill's Choppers. I think it serves as headquarters for the group. It's possible Bill might know where Ed is."

He gave us an address from his phone directory.

We piled back into the car and headed for the motorcycle shop. I hoped it wouldn't be another dead end.

CHAPTER TWENTY

Bill's Choppers appeared to be a thriving business. A variety of makes and models of cycles were lined up on the paved lot in front of the prosperous-looking showroom. Inside custom models were displayed with all kinds of bells and whistles and elaborate paint jobs. I had a feeling they cost more than most mid-sized cars. Ty seemed quite intrigued with them.

"You ever ride one of these?" I asked him.

"When I was a kid I, had a small off-road bike. Loved that thing. Unfortunately, I wrecked it and broke my leg, and my dad wouldn't let me get it fixed or get a new one. He said he couldn't afford the hospital bills if I was going to bust myself up. I don't think I was ever as mad at him as I was at that time."

"You got over it, I trust."

"It took me some years. But then I got to thinking what I would have done if I'd been in his shoes. Of course I was grown then, and had a modicum of sense. I realized I'd probably do the same thing."

"No desire to ride one now?"

"Think I'll stick with my car. That's about as much fun as I can take at my age."

While we were talking, a salesman approached us. A burley middle-aged man, he could have easily been mistaken for a Hell's Angel member. He was wearing a tee shirt with a logo for the shop on the front. He'd rolled up the sleeves to show off his arms which were tattooed from shoulder to wrist with fantastical designs so that not an inch of pink skin was visible. His head was shaved, and he wore small diamond studs in his ears and a ring in his nose. He could have walked straight out of a comic book.

"May I help you?" he asked in an unexpectedly high voice. It seemed incongruous it should come out of such a body. Maybe he felt the need for the macho look to offset the impression he made when he spoke.

"We're trying to find a guy by the name of Ed Stillman," Ty said. "We understand he rides with a group that's connected to your shop."

"Yeah? Why do you want him?"

We'd decided on our way to the shop that perhaps we shouldn't be telling everyone the real reason why we wanted to talk to Ed. They might be inclined to lie to us if we told them it was connected to a murder. That might have been our mistake all along. We were used to being honest, and honesty isn't always the best method for solving crimes. We had a lot to learn.

Ty told him what we'd agreed to say. "A relative of his has died and left him a small inheritance, but the lawyer managing the estate hasn't been able to find him. We volunteered to help because we knew the deceased."

"Well, I'm sure Ed can use it. He's had a hard time recently making ends meet. His job only pays minimum wage. He bought the bike back when he was making good money and now it's his only ride. With gas prices the way they are, it's a hell of a lot cheaper than a car."

"So can you help us?" Ty asked.

"I don't know where Ed lives. He's moved around a lot recently, bunking in with friends or whatever he can find cheap. But you're in luck 'cause today he's in an off-road race east of here with a bunch of his buddies. Tryin' to make a few extra bucks. I think he'd be very glad to see you."

I doubted that very much.

"You mean he rides a dirt bike?" Ty asked.

"It's one of those combination street and dirt bikes. Can ride it just about anywhere."

"I thought you said he was working. How can he be out racing now?" I asked.

"He works the evening shift at a convenience store."

"Tell us how to find him," Ty said.

Ty wrote down the directions on the back of a Harley Davidson sales flyer. He wrote the address of the convenience store as well in case we needed to look for him there.

Back in the car we headed east on I-40 to the next exit and wound around back roads till we finally came to a small sign beside a dirt road that said "Motocross Race Today."

The road led through a heavily wooded area for a quarter of a mile or so until suddenly we burst out into an open space. A huge dirt track had been built in the clearing with undulating turns and steep hills that dropped off sharply causing the bikes to fly off the top to land many yards away. The sound of roaring engines and the clouds of dust whipped up by the bikes assaulted our ears and eyes. Ty pulled into a flat spot next to the woods where a number of cars and trailers were parked. He put up the hard top before he got out. Pretty neat, I thought, to do that with the touch of a button. I could remember when the tops of convertibles were a lot of work to take up and down.

"Good thing I didn't get it washed recently. It's gonna be covered in dust."

"*We're* going to be covered in dust," I said. "And I may be deaf by the time we get out of here."

"Almost as loud as kids play their music these days."

We walked over to a group of spectators at the far side of the track. Most of them had brought folding chairs so they could spend the afternoon in relative comfort. I sorely wished that we had something to sit on.

We watched the bikers for a few minutes wondering why anyone would risk their necks to do this. It wasn't my idea of fun, but then caution has always been my middle name. Even as a child I was super cautious, probably the only one who couldn't (or wouldn't) do a somersault over the teeter totter support or work my way across the monkey bars at the nearby playground. As an adult I still avoid precarious pastimes. On second thought some people might think our pursuit of Ralph's killer wasn't the safest or wisest thing we could have done. So maybe I'd lost some of my childhood timidity. I hoped I hadn't stumbled into downright foolhardiness in doing so.

The roar was so loud I wasn't sure if we could make ourselves heard. Finally Ty approached a nearby onlooker and began a conversation. Because of the noise I couldn't hear what they were saying, but I assumed he was asking about Ed.

When he rejoined me he pointed out a rider on a neon green and black bike who had just made a sharp turn and was climbing the hill nearest us.

"That's Ed," he said nearly shouting to be heard. "They say this race will last about another twenty or thirty minutes. Then we should be able to talk to him."

"Okay," I hollered back. "Hope I can still hear by then."

So we waited patiently as the bikes flew around the course as though being pursued by demons. Maybe the riders had their own personal demons, and this was a way to exorcize them. I could only wonder.

Fifteen minutes later as Ed's bike came roaring around the turn nearest us and began to climb the hill, he seemed to lose control, and the machine veered to the left putting him into the path of an oncoming bike. The other driver jerked hard to the right trying to miss him and lost control of his own machine. Both riders were thrown, Ed to the left of the nearest hill so he fell in between two sections of the raceway. The other rider was ejected onto the grass strip beside the track narrowly missing spectators. He lay there dazed for a couple of minutes as a few of the onlookers rushed to help him. Then he slowly rose as one of them gave him a hand. He didn't seem to be seriously hurt for he was eager to check on the condition of his bike.

A couple of men who were sitting near us ran to the side of the track, and once they'd made sure it was safe, crossed over to where Ed had been flung. All spectators were on their feet now in concern as the other bikers continued on. Apparently the riders were used to accidents that involved minor scrapes and bruises. They thought it was all part of the spectacle and not sufficient reason to stop the race.

We couldn't see what was happening with Ed as the hill obscured the area where he fell. But shortly one of the men came back across the track and picked up a case with a Red Cross emblem on it. I thought this couldn't be good news.

Finally, someone in charge realized the gravity of the situation and stopped the race. After the ear-splitting din the cycles made, the sudden silence was startling. But it wasn't too long before we heard a shrill siren filling the air with short bursts of noise and saw an ambulance emerge from the entrance road into the clearing.

Everyone was subdued as they watched the EMTs clamber from the ambulance as soon as it stopped, two of them maneuvering a gurney up and over the closest dirt track to the other side.

"This doesn't look good," I said to Ty.

"You're right. Not for him or for us. I don't think he'll be in any shape to question."

"Should we just leave?"

"I'd like to know where they're taking him. Perhaps find out something about his condition."

It was another twenty or thirty minutes before we saw them roll the gurney back over the track with a prone figure strapped down with a neck brace, back board and oxygen mask. As soon as he was rolled into the ambulance, the race officials came over to where the spectators waited. The entire crowd seemed tense waiting for news that seemed destined to be dire.

"How's Ed?" one of the men shouted as they approached.

"It's pretty bad," said the man in front who seemed to be in charge. "He might have broke his neck. He was unconscious so we don't know for sure."

"Where are they taking him?" Ty asked.

The man looked at Ty with curiosity. "Do I know you?" he asked.

"No. I came here to meet him. I had some business to discuss with him."

"Well, I don't think he's going to be discussin' anything any time soon. They took him to UNC hospital, but y'all gonna waste your time goin' there today. Might be a while before he'll be talkin' to you."

Others began to pepper him with questions. Ty nodded his head toward the car and said to me "We might as well leave. We're not going to find out anything more here."

CHAPTER TWENTY-ONE

The ride home was far less upbeat than the drive over had been a couple of hours earlier. It looked as if our last lead had fizzled out right under our noses. We didn't know if Ed's injuries were life-threatening or not. We couldn't very well interview him if he was in serious or critical condition. Once he left the hospital we might not be able to track him down again. It didn't seem likely he'd be going back to riding his motorcycle any time soon, and no one we'd talked to seemed to know where he lived.

It was about four o'clock when we arrived back at GH. As we entered the building I said, "Let's go see if Justine's home and find out how Phyllis is doing."

We went to her apartment and knocked on the door but no one answered.

"She may still be at the hospital," I said. "I wish we could find out what Phyllis's condition is, but we won't get squat out of the staff here because of the patient privacy laws. I can understand why they have them, but it sure can be frustrating."

"We can always go visit Phyllis ourselves. Want to go after dinner?"

"Let's do."

I decided to get in a few laps in the pool before dinner. Spunky's office is next to the pool so I dropped in to say hi before I swam. She had her ear to the ground around GH, and sometimes I could get her to tell me little bits of information that I normally wouldn't hear. She definitely was not a gossip monger, and she never said anything negative about the residents, but she would share harmless details that she heard second hand.

"I don't suppose you've heard anything about Phyllis, have you?" I asked.

"Actually I have. I ran into Justine in the lobby as she came back from the hospital. She says Phyllis is doing okay physically, but she's pretty depressed. I guess that's not too surprising though."

So Justine wasn't at the hospital with Phyllis. Probably out running errands.

"Does Glendon Hills have anyone who could counsel her?" I asked.

"No one on staff. But I imagine her doctor will set her up with a psychologist."

"I hope so. The next time she tries to do something like that it could be fatal."

"So have you and Ty had any success with looking into Ralph's background?"

"We've talked to people where he used to work. He certainly didn't endear himself to his coworkers or his bosses. Seems he stole customers away from other salesmen and padded prices to the customers so he could pocket some of the money. Not a nice guy overall."

Spunky grimaced. "You've got to wonder why she stayed with him."

"I think she was scared to leave him. She has very little self confidence as you probably know and didn't know how to extricate herself from the relationship."

Spunky didn't say anything for a minute or two. I got the impression that she was trying to decide whether to confide in me or not.

Finally she said, "I'm not in a position to tell you some things I know. But I can tell you this. You might want to talk to some of the other residents who live near the Duncans. I don't think all of Ralph's misbehavior was confined to his work places."

"Thanks, Spunky. I hadn't thought to do that."

I went on to the pool and swam a number of laps. It felt so good I didn't realize how late it was and had to hurry through my shower to get to the dining room in time to meet Ty.

Over dinner I told him about my conversation with Spunky. "Justine wasn't visiting Phyllis when we knocked on her door. She must have gone somewhere else. Spunky saw her earlier in the lobby as she came back from the hospital."

"So how is Phyllis doing?"

"Okay physically. Not so good mentally."

"I'm sure they'll get her some psychological help over there."

"Spunky said something kind of strange to me. She told me it wasn't anything she could talk about, but she advised me to question some of the other residents on your hall. Apparently they will have something to say about Ralph."

"Hmmm. That's interesting. You'd think I'd be aware of anything happening on my hall, but maybe I've missed something."

"Well, you don't spend a lot of time in your apartment during the day. You're usually out and about somewhere, so you can't know about everything that goes on there."

"We could do that tomorrow if you'd like," Ty said. "Are we still going to the hospital this evening?"

"Sure. Maybe we can cheer Phyllis up a little."

"Speaking of cheering up, I had a phone message from my cousin Perry. Talk about someone being down in the dumps. He's had no success finding a kidney donor, and I guess his health gets a little worse every day."

I had succeeded in putting him out of my mind temporarily, but now I was faced with the question of what I was going to do about the fact I had a blood type compatible with Perry's.

I must have looked stricken.

"Vi? Is something wrong?"

I hadn't wanted to share this information with anybody, but now, with Perry's health deteriorating, I needed to discuss it with someone.

"You remember when he said he had O type blood? That was when you knew you couldn't be a donor. Well I do have O blood."

Ty didn't say anything for a minute. He looked at me with sympathy. "I know what you must be feeling," he finally said. "I was so resistant to the idea of having surgery, particularly for someone I didn't know. I can't tell you how relieved I was to find out I wasn't compatible."

"I can't tell you how shocked I was to find out I *was* compatible."

"There's nothing that says this is something you have to do."

"I know. But how would I feel if he died, and I knew I might have been able to help him?"

"That's a tough one, Vi."

"Well, I guess the only thing I can do is to sleep on it."

We turned the discussion to something else to my relief.

After dinner we drove to the hospital, stopping at a super market on the way to pick up a small bouquet of flowers in a glass vase.

Babs Osborn was there when we arrived. She was the one we had called to console Ginger when Lester died. She was known to visit most of our residents when they were hospitalized which was frequently considering the age and state of health of many of them.

Phyllis looked tired and pale in the bed, her wrists wrapped in gauze. Babs was telling her a funny story about an incident in the dining room. Phyllis made an attempt to smile, but it wasn't very convincing.

"Hey, Phyllis, you're looking good," Ty said heartily. He was good at telling lies with a straight face.

"How are they treating you?" I set the flowers on her bedside table.

She shrugged. "Were you the ones who found me?" she asked.

"We were. You scared the daylights out of me," I said.

"Next time I'll be sure my door is locked."

I was almost speechless. "Phyllis, there isn't going to be a next time. You have too much to live for. Everybody is rooting for you."

"That's what I've been telling her," Babs said. "She needs to get well so she can participate in some of our activities. She can join the book club or learn to knit or how to play Mah Jongg."

Unless they send her off to jail.

That reminded me I had missed Mah Jongg that afternoon. My mind had been on Phyllis, and I'd completely forgotten about it. I was missing out on things in order to exonerate Phyllis so she *could* participate. If Phyllis had no desire to go on living, our efforts were in vain..

"You might want to join a grief support group," I said to her. "Everyone needs help to get over the death of a loved one. I know others at GH who've found it very helpful."

Phyllis's eyes filled with tears. "It isn't just the fact that Ralph died. It's that I probably caused it."

"Nonsense!" Ty said. "None of us believes that for a minute. You've got to get that idea out of your mind."

We steered the conversation to other less emotional topics and tried our darnedest to get a smile from her. We didn't succeed with that but she did seem a little less morose by the time we left.

The three of us left the hospital together. Babs told us that her doctor had brought in a psychologist to work with her, and she probably wouldn't be released until they were fairly certain she wouldn't harm herself again. They had started her on an anti-depressant but it takes a while for it to take hold.

"You do such a good job helping out our residents," I said to her in the elevator. "I was grateful when you talked to Ginger after Lester died."

"That was one of the stranger situations I've gotten involved in," she said. "She was as upset over that bird as most people are over losing a spouse. She told me some other things too. Since I'm not employed now but only trying to voluntarily help residents in trouble, I feel that I can share some things I know if it's in their best interests."

"No client-counselor privilege you mean," Ty said.

"Right. Ginger told me that Ralph had come on to her a couple of times. Shortly after the Duncans moved in, Ginger's TV started acting up. She thought Ralph might know if it was because she hit the wrong buttons on the remote. You know how that sometimes happens, and you can't figure out how to undo it."

"I've done it myself," I said. "Ty got me back on track."

"I guess a lot of us aren't very tech savvy around GH. Talk about teaching old dogs new tricks," Babs said. "Anyway, she said he was very fresh with her, but she wouldn't be specific about what he did. I guess she was too embarrassed."

I wondered if that was what Spunky was referring to when she suggested I talk to the residents on that hall.

We parted with Babs in the parking lot. When we got back to GH I was ready for bed. I was physically and emotionally drained by the events of the day.

CHAPTER TWENTY-TWO

It was another almost sleepless night. So much was weighing on my mind that I couldn't stop the thoughts from churning like a washing machine on steroids. What kind of shape was Ed Stillman in? Was Phyllis going to try and kill herself again? What about Perry? Should I tell him I have O positive blood and get tested to see if I would be compatible? I finally took a couple of melatonin tablets, and they helped me unwind enough I dozed off about 3 am. After what Phyllis told me about her sleeping pills, I wasn't about to try them. I might put on even more weight if I got up in the night and raided the refrigerator unaware of what I was doing.

Ty and I had decided the night before that we needed a break from all the depressing things that we'd been involved in. He suggested we take a trip to the North Carolina Zoo, and I readily agreed. I had heard a lot of good things about it but hadn't had a chance to go there.

Luckily the day was unusually warm for late March. It was about a forty-minute drive to the zoo which is located in the center of the state near the little town of Seagrove known for its plethora of potters. Another trip I'd like to take sometime.

The African exhibit with the elephants, giraffes, and other animals indigenous to the African continent was closed for the winter months, but the North American exhibit was open. Since the zoo is comprised of five hundred acres, I realized it would be difficult to take everything in on one trip, so half of it was more than enough for us. From polar bears to alligators, arctic foxes, elk and bison we saw just about every kind of animal that roams our part of the world as well as snakes and amphibious creatures too. I loved the aviary most of all. For one thing it was as warm as a summer day in the glass-enclosed space that's filled with exotic trees and flowers and inhabited by many bird species. It was a challenge to spy them amongst the jungle-like foliage as their bird songs filled the air. They could briefly be spotted between branches of the giant spiral ginger, palms, weeping fig, and West Indian mahogany trees (thank goodness for labels). The most amazing birds were the scarlet ibis which would congregate in bunches of five or six, their gorgeous plumage reflected in the small artificial stream that flows through the exhibit. Other beautiful birds were the golden-crested mynah, red-capped cardinal, and the golden white-eye which is critically endangered.

It was a wonderful day, and it took our minds off of all the troublesome events of the past couple of weeks. On the way home we stopped off in Asheboro to have supper at a German restaurant, and we both ordered wiener schnitzel, German potato salad, and kraut, a treat we never get at GH. Even Ty couldn't resist the German chocolate cake for dessert.

When we got back to GH we decided to talk to the residents on Ty's floor the next afternoon. Sunday is always a leisurely day and not much is offered in the way of entertainment. So we hoped to find them at home.

The first apartment we went to was that of Buck and Gladys Barlow who live at the far end of the hall. The Barlows are probably the most attractive couple at GH. Gladys is tall and slim and her appearance is always impeccable. She even manages to be stylish in exercise class where the majority of us are pretty slovenly in our thrown-together outfits. I'll wear anything that's loose and comfortable whether it matches or not while Gladys could have just stepped off the runway for designer sports outfits. Her honey-blond hair looks as natural as it can get on a seventy-four-year-old, and she wouldn't appear in public unless her makeup is carefully applied and her manicure is perfect.

Buck is the perfect foil for Gladys. His handsome face is framed by thick white hair that plays up his year-round tan acquired from playing tennis. His six-foot frame is well toned and even the most casual wear looks like a million dollars on him.

Gladys answered the door and invited us in. Theirs is one of the largest apartments in the building. The units vary from a one-bedroom, small den, and one-bath model of about eight hundred square feet like mine to ones like the Barlow's which has three bedrooms, two baths and is over sixteen hundred square feet. Buck had been a bigwig in the furniture industry in nearby High Point so I'm sure they could easily afford it. The "buy-in" price of the apartments is based on size as is the monthly fee that covers everything from meals, housekeeping service, utilities, use of all the many amenities and of course the extras like entertainment, exercise classes, craft classes, bus trips and so on. I can just barely afford mine which is the lowest in the building.

The apartment is beautifully furnished which isn't surprising since he was connected with the industry. It made mine look like a dump in comparison. Rather than pay to have my household furnishings brought down from New York State, I decided to donate most of it to Goodwill before I left. Not that I had anything fine. Much of it was passed down from other generations, and by that I don't mean fine antiques but more like thirties' and forties' nondescript pieces. I didn't have an emotional attachment to any of the pieces which were mostly pretty ugly even to my undiscerning eye. When I moved into GH I furnished it with pieces bought at consignment shops in the area. Interior design is not my thing, and as long as I have a comfortable chair to sit in and bed to lie in I'm happy.

"Sorry that Buck isn't here," Gladys said. "He had some errands to run. But it's so nice to have you visit. Can I get you something to drink? Coffee? Iced tea?"

We both declined. "Maybe it's just as well that Buck isn't here," I said, "because we'd like to ask you a personal question. You don't have to answer if you're uncomfortable about it. But we're trying to help Phyllis out. She's in a precarious situation."

We hadn't discussed the Duncans with anyone at GH except for Spunky and Justine because we wanted to keep a low profile. But the story had been in the paper about Phyllis being charged in Ralph's death so there had to be a lot of talk going around. We decided we needed to find out what was being said.

"Oh, there is so much speculation about her," Gladys said. "None of us knows the real story about Ralph's death, so you can imagine some of the wild tales going around. I understand she's in the hospital. Do you know why she's there and how she is?"

"We saw her last night," Ty said. "Physically she's doing okay, but we're worried about her mental condition. All that she's been through has pushed her right to the edge. She attempted to take her own life by slashing her wrists."

"Oh my god, what a shame. You know even though we're neighbors here we hardly knew her because she kept so much to herself. Now Ralph, he was something else."

"What exactly do you mean by that?" I asked.

"I think he came on to every woman on this hall. We all tried to steer clear of him if we possibly could. He was the real life 'dirty old man.'"

"And how did Buck react to that?" Ty asked.

"He told him he'd punch his lights out if he didn't stay away from me," she said with a smile. "To tell you the truth I was proud of him. Buck's a very soft spoken man, and he hardly ever gets mad. I was delighted that he stood up to him."

"Did Ralph bother you after that?" I asked.

"No. I guess he took Buck at his word. That was about six months ago, and he seemed to go out of his way to avoid me after that."

There wasn't much else she could tell us about the Duncans so we thanked her for being so candid and left.

Once we were out in the hall, we whispered so our voices wouldn't carry. "It sounds like there wasn't any recent confrontation between Buck and Ralph. If we take her at her word, we could scratch his name off our list," I said.

"Yeah, I agree. So that eliminates three out of the five couples or singles on this hall including Ginger, and I can't imagine her stabbing anyone. Buck seemed to have scared Ralph off from flirting with his wife some time ago, and then there's me," said Ty.

"That leaves Heidi Manning and the Christophers."

"Right. Should we talk to Heidi? I've been thinking it might have been a jealous husband who did it, and she's a widow."

"Well, if he got terribly out of line, I can see the possibility of a woman wanting to kill him," I said.

Ty looked a little skeptical. "If she were young and strong maybe she could have done it. But Heidi is in her late eighties and pretty frail. I think he could have easily disarmed her."

"Who's to say she doesn't have a boyfriend?"

"Around here the news would be all over the place. It would not go unnoticed."

I shrugged. "You're probably right, but it can't hurt to talk to her, can it?"

"Sure."

When we rang Heidi's doorbell it took a couple of minutes for her to answer it. Heidi is one of those sweet-faced old ladies whose laugh lines are permanently etched in her face and her thin pewter-colored flyaway hair resembles cotton candy. She's the Norman Rockwell image of what a grandmother is supposed to look like. In fact she played Mrs. Santa Claus at our Christmas party last year. I was surprised to see she was using a walker now. This made Ty's argument even more viable, but as long as we were here, I figured we might as well see what she had to say about Ralph.

"What a nice surprise," she said when she saw us.

"We just wondered if we could talk to you for a few minutes," I said.

"Of course," she said smiling and opened the door wide. I think she was lonely and glad to have visitors. I hoped we wouldn't disappoint her when she found out what we were here for.

We preceded her into the living room and settled in on her sofa. I noticed how slowly she made her way.

"How are you doing Heidi?" I asked.

"I had a little fall last week, but I didn't break anything thank goodness. But the doctor suggested I use a walker because my balance is so bad."

"I'm sorry to hear that," I said.

She waved her hand. "No big deal. These old legs aren't what they used to be. I'm just glad I can still get around even if I have to push this buggy to get there."

She always had been one of the more upbeat residents, and it seemed she wasn't going to let a little setback get her down. I admired her so much.

"So what is it you wanted to talk about?"

"We wondered if you could tell us anything about the Duncans. Since you live next door to them, we thought maybe you would know more about them than the rest of us did."

"Why are you asking?"

Heidi had never been one of those who thrived on rumors. I'd seen her walk away from a group if she considered the conversation out of line.

"I'm sure you've read about Phyllis being accused of killing Ralph. We think they've got it all wrong and are trying to come up with anything that can help her," Ty explained.

"I see. I wouldn't normally talk about my neighbors. But under the circumstances, I guess it's all right. Even though the walls are fairly soundproof, I could hear Ralph yelling now and then. It was muffled so I couldn't understand what he said. But it sounded pretty scary. I often wondered if I should do something about it like report it to the management."

"But you didn't?" Ty asked.

"Honestly I was kind of scared to. I didn't know what he might do if he found out I was the one who reported it. I guess it was a big mistake not to have done something."

"I very much doubt it would have made a difference," I said.

"Thank you for saying that, Vi. It has been weighing on my mind. But there's something else that happened which I wouldn't normally talk about, but I guess I should tell you."

"What's that?"

She was looking uncomfortable now. "Promise me this won't get around the building."

"It won't get past our lips unless it would turn out to be something that could exonerate Phyllis," Ty answered. "In that case we would share it only with her lawyer ."

She was stroking her chin trying to get up the courage to speak. She was someone who didn't get the least bit of pleasure out of being indiscreet.

"It must have been a day or two before Ralph died. I opened my door to get the newspaper. I normally get up pretty early and read the paper while I drink my coffee and eat my cereal. At that very minute I saw Ralph coming out of the Christopher's apartment. He was looking very shifty, and he sort of did a double take when he saw me. I didn't wait to speak to him or see where he was going. I hurriedly shut my door and locked it."

"What time was it?" I asked.

"Around eight. And the thing that shocked me so was that Bill Christopher had gone off on a fishing trip and Tootsie was alone."

CHAPTER TWENTY-THREE

When we left Heidi's apartment we decided to go to the café for coffee.

"So what do you think?" Ty asked.

I knew immediately what he was referring to. "Do you think Tootsie Christopher could have had an affair with Ralph?" I asked. The idea seemed preposterous to me. Why would an accomplished woman like her want to have anything to do with him?

"It's hard to imagine. It also makes it very awkward to talk to them. Obviously we'd have to split the Christophers up. And I can't believe Tootsie would admit it if it were true."

"You know, I could invite Tootsie to my apartment so I could talk to her privately. She's chair of the dining committee, and I'll tell her I want to discuss some issues in the dining room."

"You going to tell her that they should quit serving Brussels sprouts?" he asked with a grin.

"That and liver. I'll have to figure out a way to question her without offending her. It ain't gonna be easy."

We each went back to our own apartments so I could make the call. I was feeling very uncomfortable about it but willed myself to carry on.

When Tootsie answered the phone I told her I had some suggestions for the dining committee and asked if she would she mind coming to my apartment to talk about it.

"I'm expecting an important phone call," I said with my fingers crossed, "so I don't want to leave for fear I'll miss it."

She agreed to come, so as soon as I hung up I hurriedly picked up the Sunday paper from the floor and tidied the kitchen where I'd left dirty dishes in the sink. I've become lax about keeping my place visitor ready. I figure at my age I should be able to be a bit of a slob, and I don't entertain except for my niece and her husband. She's aware of my lack of housekeeping skills but it doesn't seem to bother her. Besides when we're together, we spend most of the time in the dining room. Living here has freed me from the anxiety over what to fix for dinner when I have guests. That's one of the best perks as far as I'm concerned. Let the staff do the planning as well as the cooking.

About ten minutes later Tootsie was at the door. I'll never know how she got her moniker, but I've found that Southern women often have the most unconventional names. They usually start as nicknames when they are young but stick for life. Somehow calling an eighty-something woman Tootsie seems a little ludicrous.

I invited her in, and she strode into my living room full of bluster and self importance. She is one of the most active residents, and is the kind that immediately takes charge of any group she is in. Her brown hair doesn't have a hint of gray, though I couldn't be sure if it was natural or not. She stood stiffly erect, no dowager hump for her. She's quite athletic and participates in the Senior Games in golf and bowling. She's complained to Spunky that our exercises are much too easy, and whatever Spunky asks us to do, Tootsie will do it twice as fast or figure out some way to make it more difficult. The others just think she is showing off, but I believe the woman is addicted to exercise. She can't seem to sit still for very long, and I see her outside jogging around the building, or going up and down the inside stairs as fast as she can while the rest of us use the elevators.

"So, you have some kind of gripe about the dining room?" she asked before I barely sat down. I had wanted to lead the conversation but decided it might not be possible with Tootsie.

"I have several. First the room is always too cold. I have to remember to bring a sweater or jacket or I freeze to death."

"You're about the fiftieth person who's complained about that. I've talked to the staff several times, but it seems that it's difficult to regulate the temperature, especially in such a large space. I guess you'll just have to continue to wear something warm." She didn't seem the least sympathetic. Maybe her own internal thermostat was turned up higher than mine. "What else?"

"Do they have to put a sauce or gravy of some kind on every thing they fix? I have to get larger clothes about every four or five months."

"Ask the servers to tell the kitchen to leave off the sauce," she said impatiently. "That's not so hard is it?"

Oh boy, I was glad I didn't have to deal with this lady very often. "Most of the dishes are prepared with the sauce or gravy so it can't be left off."

She shrugged her shoulders. "Guess you'll just have to eat less then."

You'd think the head of a committee could be a little more approachable. Not Tootsie. She was going to shoot down any complaint I had. How was I ever going to ask her about Ralph if she was so uncooperative about suggestions for the dining room?

I tried going at it from an oblique angle. "It wasn't just the dining room I wanted to talk about. I'm trying to do what I can to help out Phyllis Duncan."

"If that isn't a fine mess. Why didn't she just leave him? I'll never understand women who let men walk all over them. She didn't have to be a door mat." She considered that remark and then added with a half smile, "Well, I guess she wasn't being a door mat when she stuck that knife in him."

She didn't tiptoe around about it, nor did she express any sympathy for Phyllis. It would be difficult to appeal to her softer side since there didn't appear to be one. I'm quite sure *she* was not a door mat.

"I feel quite sure she didn't do it," I said. "She just happened to take the fall for it because she picked up the knife."

"Why on earth would she do that? Doesn't she ever watch *Law and Order*? You're never supposed to mess with the evidence."

"She wasn't thinking about that when she found Ralph on the floor covered in blood. She thought the murderer might still be there and she picked it up to defend herself."

"Well, obviously that was a bad move. She should have just gotten out of the apartment as fast as she could."

"Tootsie, what can you tell me about Ralph? Did you know him very well?"

She looked at me sharply with a scowl on her face. "Why would I know him well?"

"Because you lived near him. Since you were neighbors, I thought you might have gotten together."

For the first time she seemed uncomfortable, not anxious to speak her mind. After a big sigh she said, "I didn't know him any better than anyone else here did. They never invited any of their neighbors over. Since Ralph was so outgoing, I thought it was Phyllis who didn't want to have company."

"Did you ever try to entertain them?"

"I asked them over once when they first moved in. They turned me down with some lame excuse. I didn't try again."

I had to work up the courage to ask the next question. I figured I would land on her shit list once I did. "What if I told you someone saw Ralph coming out of your place early one morning? And this was when your husband was away."

Her face turned red, and I was afraid she might go up in flames any minute. "My god, do they have a bunch of spies around here? I can't believe this!"

I shrugged. "You know how it is. Stories get around." I didn't really think that Heidi had told anyone else, but it served my purpose to let Tootsie think so.

She stood up in a huff, eyes blazing, chin raised high. "I called Ralph one morning to help me move a heavy piece of furniture. I knew it would take maintenance a week to get around to it. If everyone wants to make something out of it, then let them." She stomped over to my door and let herself out without another word.

CHAPTER TWENTY-FOUR

❝Moving furniture at eight o'clock in the morning?" I said to Ty at dinner that night. "That seems pretty far-fetched to me."

Since it was Sunday we had gone out to Panera's for supper again.

"I guess it's up to me to talk to Bill. But I can't figure out how to do it subtly. I can't go up to him and ask if he thinks Tootsie was having an affair with Ralph. That would stir up a hornet's nest. Any ideas how I can go about this?"

"You know, Cora Lee Hillman seems to have an inside track to just about everything that goes on around GH. Let's talk to her before we go any further with this. If anyone knows it'll be Cora Lee."

"I'll let you do it. She'll probably open up more to you."

"I hate to get her started because she can be fairly vicious sometimes, but she usually is right. She must have a whole bevy of informants to know so much."

I agreed to call upon Cora Lee in the morning. I really didn't want to deal with the Duncans' tragedy any more that day. It was getting to be such a downer.

We were walking into the building when we ran into Justine who was also coming from the parking lot. She looked terrible: pale, exhausted, and extremely sad.

I was alarmed by her appearance. "What's the matter, Justine? Is Phyllis worse?" I assumed she'd come from visiting Phyllis at the hospital. I knew I was overdue for a visit and planned to see her in the morning.

"No. It's my nephew," she said, collapsing into a rocking chair that graced the reception area. I sat down on the love seat next to her. "He was in a terrible motorbike accident over near Chapel Hill on Friday. He's in bad shape. I don't know whether he's going to make it or not."

"Good lord. Do you mean Ed Stillman?" I asked. Surely there couldn't have been more than one serious motorbike accident in that area on Friday. I couldn't believe the coincidence.

She looked at me in astonishment. "You know Ed?"

"We never got to meet him. We were told by the owner of the motorcycle shop he frequented that he was in the race on Friday, so we went over to the track to speak to him. But, unfortunately, he crashed before we had a chance to get up with him. We had no idea how badly he was hurt."

"We tracked him down because he'd worked with Ralph Duncan," Ty said, obviously as surprised as I was at this turn of events. He sat in a chair opposite Justine. "We've been looking up anyone who worked with or knew Ralph before he moved here. How did it happen they worked together?"

"When Ralph was looking for a job, I told him my nephew had said there was an opening at the fence company. He applied and got the job. I'm not sure why I helped him out except I wanted to get him out of Phyllis's hair. He was even worse when he was around the house all day and frustrated because he wasn't working."

"I understand there was some bad blood between Ed and Ralph," I said. "We were told Ralph stole customers from Ed and then quoted them prices too high and pocketed some of the difference. In fact we were told Ed quit because of what Ralph had done."

"That's not really true. He and Ralph were far from being buddies, but Ed didn't quit because of him. He just decided he didn't like sales work. I think Ray, the owner, exaggerated Ralph's so-called misdeeds. Don't get me wrong, I didn't like Ralph one bit. But I think most of the employees tried to take over each other's customers. It was part of the company culture and led to general unhappiness. Ray didn't keep very good control of things and morale was low."

"So he quit without having another job lined up?" Ty asked. "Not too smart."

"It was at the very start of the economic bust. He had no idea that times were going to get so bad. He ended up working for a convenience store, but he's single and he's been able to get by. He's mostly interested in motorcycles, and that's what's kept him going. As long as he can ride, he's happy."

"How tragic it led to this," I said. "How badly is he injured?"

"He broke his neck. It was a fluke. They don't normally have such serious accidents at those races. But somehow he fell wrong, and it was a devastating injury."

"I'm so sorry," I said.

"I'm his closest relative," Justine said, tears welling in her eyes. "His dad, my oldest brother, died a few years ago, and his mother disappeared when he was young. So I'm the one who has to oversee his care. I don't know whether I can handle it or not. There may be some really tough decisions to make down the road."

"That is a daunting responsibility," Ty said. "Perhaps you could talk to Reverend Bill about it."

"Thanks, Ty. That's a good suggestion," she said, pulling out a tissue from her purse and wiping her eyes.

Poor Justine. First her sister-in-law dies, her best friend is accused of murder, and shortly after her nephew is critically hurt. What a catastrophic series of events to endure.

We all parted company and went to our separate apartments. As I lay in bed later that evening I thought of all the people in the building who were dealing with tragedies. There's nothing like a retirement home to magnify all of life's adversities. At our age, we face the worst that life can throw at us. Whether we sink or swim is determined largely by our accumulated experiences and how we've responded to them. Have we been able to withstand the random blows that have knocked us down along the way? Or have we folded under pressure? Surprisingly, most seem to have a resilience that has been honed by the vicissitudes of living and bear up under pressures you would think would crush them.

The next morning after exercise Ty and I headed to the hospital to visit Phyllis. If Justine had spent the weekend with her nephew then Phyllis had probably been alone. I was anxious to see how she was doing.

She was dozing in bed when we entered her room. The heavy bandages were off her wrists and small gauze patches covered the wounds. She still looked thin and pale.

I touched her lightly on the shoulder. "Phyllis?" I said softly so I wouldn't startle her.

She opened her eyes and blinked as if she wasn't sure who I was. Then she gave me a feeble attempt at a smile. "Hi Vi. Good to see you. It's been kind of lonesome here," she said. "I can't believe Justine hasn't been to see me in several days. Do you know where she is?"

"Her nephew was badly hurt racing a motorcycle over near Chapel Hill," I said. "She's been at the hospital over there."

"Do you mean Ed Stillman?"

"That's right. Do you know him?" Ty asked.

"Sure. He worked with Ralph at Fantana Fencing. And I'd met him a time or two when he was at Justine's."

"Do you know what kind of a relationship Ralph and Ed had? I've heard two different stories," I asked.

"Relationship? I don't know. Ralph usually didn't get along with his coworkers. He always complained about them, no matter where he worked. I got so tired of hearing him grouse I kind of tuned him out and didn't pay much attention. So, no matter who it was, if he worked with Ralph, there was probably some bad blood."

That wasn't the most helpful statement. But if Ed was as badly injured as Justine indicated, his relationship to Ralph was a moot point now.

We stayed a little while longer and chatted. It was up to Ty and me to keep the conversation going as Phyllis seemed to have spent all her energy talking about Ed. I hoped that the psychiatrists and antidepressants were going to help her although I knew it took time. It was obvious she had a way to go yet before she would be ready to live alone again.

"So," Ty said on our way back to GH, "where do you think we stand at this point?"

"I'd say so far it looks as if we've struck out," I said. "We seem to be getting nowhere fast."

CHAPTER TWENTY-FIVE

Ty planned to play with the Bridge Dudes that afternoon, so I called our resident busybody Cora Lee to see if we could meet. She was on her way to play Hand and Foot but said she'd be free around three. We agreed to meet in the café for coffee.

That seemed like the perfect opportunity to go to the pool and spend ten minutes in the whirlpool/spa afterward. It got a lot of the kinks out.

Cora Lee was waiting for me when I got to the café. A tall thin woman she has the figure that models crave and always looks smashing in her fashionable outfits that undoubtedly cost big bucks. The only thing that spoils the picture is the face that has been "lifted" once too often and now looks like a grim mask that shows no emotion because it has been pulled so taut it can't. I will say the dye job that keeps her hair an auburn shade was well done.

"You wanted to ask me something?" she asked as I joined her in a booth after pouring myself a cup of decaf.

"Yes, I know you've got your ear to the ground around here, and I thought you might be able to answer a question for me." I hoped I had stated it in a way that wouldn't offend her. I wouldn't want to get on her bad side.

She looked at me with a frown for a minute without speaking, and I was beginning to worry I'd insulted her. "So I guess I have a reputation around here as being a gossip."

"No, no," I protested, although it was true. "You're just the kind of person everyone wants to confide in. I envy you that." I hoped I hadn't overdone it.

She smiled, as much as her taut face would allow. "I do pride myself on being available to anyone who wants a shoulder to cry on."

"That's exactly what I meant." I said taking a sip of coffee to suppress my involuntary grimace. "My question is about Tootsie."

"Oh sure. Dear Tootsie." There was a distinct coolness in her voice.

I wasn't sure how she meant the "dear," but it sounded a little suspect to me. Was there some rivalry or bad blood? I wished I had more of the inside track on these relationships. I hated doing this because I was afraid it might start a rumor that could get out of hand, and I certainly didn't want to do that.

"This is strictly between the two of us," I said for what that was worth. "I just wondered if you've heard of any hint about something going on between Tootsie and Ralph Duncan."

She thought about it for a minute. "I don't think so. Ralph was always on the make, but I can't imagine any woman here would have been interested in him. To my knowledge, Tootsie had just as much disdain for him as everyone else. Whatever made you ask such a thing?"

"Someone had suggested to me that there might have been a relationship."

"I can ask around if you want me to."

"No, please don't do that. I'll take your word for it." I knew if she even asked the question, it would grow into something out of control.

"Well, okay. But I'd be happy to do a little digging."

I bet she would. "Thanks, no. It's not necessary." I prayed I hadn't started something I couldn't stop.

"By the way," she said giving me an inquiring look. "I see you and Tyrone together a lot. Is there more to this than meets the eye?"

I knew what she meant, and I wanted to put a stop to any speculation. "Ty and I are good friends. We are not romantically involved if that's what you're asking."

She gave me a sardonic grin. "Okay. If you say so."

"I say so."

She sipped her coffee while giving me the eye. "Anything else I can do for you?"

"No thanks. You've been very helpful, Cora Lee." I wondered if this had been a big mistake on my part.

"Any time."

We parted at that point, and I knew she didn't believe me for a minute. It upset me briefly, but then I decided what the heck. Let them think what they want. It might even be to our advantage.

When I got back to my apartment I had a phone message from Greta.

"Can you and Ty come to dinner tonight? Cliff is anxious to talk to you."

I phoned her back.

"I'd love to come, Greta. Always enjoy visiting you guys. But what's the urgency?"

"I've no idea. He just called me from the office and said be sure to get you two over here."

"Sounds daunting."

"Would the fact I'll be having fresh asparagus and fresh strawberry shortcake help?"

"Absolutely."

I had to go down to the lounge where the Bridge Dudes played to tell Ty about the phone call. I always hated to interrupt because they took the game so seriously. I waited till they finished a hand to whisper in his ear.

"What time?" he asked.

"Six o'clock."

"We'd better leave here about a quarter of."

I waved to them all as I left.

We met in the lobby at five-forty-five. The sky looked threatening so he left the top up on the car though I know it always spoiled the trip for him when he had to do so.

"Did you bring an umbrella?" he asked. He knew I had a small folding one I sometimes carried in my purse.

"Didn't think of it."

"I have one in the trunk if we need it."

He carried it along when we went to the house.

Greta greeted us with her usual enthusiasm and led us to the living room. Cliff was watching the news but turned the TV off when we entered. "How are you?" he asked politely though he seemed subdued, not his usual engaging self.

He took our drink orders though he knew by heart what we always had. When we all had our drinks in hand I asked, "I understand you're eager to talk to us, Cliff. What's going on?"

"I was going to bring this up later after we'd eaten. But since you asked, we'll talk now. Why on earth didn't you tell me about Phyllis's attempted suicide?"

I looked at Ty; Ty looked at me and shrugged. "It didn't occur to me, Cliff," I said. But I was beginning to realize what a mistake I'd made.

"How do you expect me to handle this case if I don't know what's going on with my client? This is a very big deal." I'd never seen Cliff this upset.

"She's doing okay," Ty said. "She's getting psychological help in the hospital, and her wounds weren't that bad."

"This could be the basis for my case," Cliff said. He waved his drink in the air with an annoyed look on his face. "Can't you see that?"

"Not really," I said. I was feeling pretty annoyed myself.

"I want to have her declared incompetent to stand trial. I think that's the best way to go. Otherwise she might have to spend the rest of her life in prison."

"Oh, so you think it's better to spend the rest of her life in a mental institution even though she doesn't belong there?" I was working up steam now. I'd never been angry with Cliff before, but I was getting more upset by the minute. Couldn't he see that the woman was innocent?

"Vi, I love you to death, but you don't know that much about law. Please leave the legal stuff to me."

I was so worked up now I knew if I opened my mouth again I would say something I'd regret later. It took all the willpower I had, but I didn't say another word about Phyllis or the case.

Greta hurriedly served dinner, probably to end the discussion. We all tried to carry on a polite conversation as we ate, but none of us had our hearts in it. We left as soon after the meal as we could without being overtly rude. I hoped our relationship hadn't been damaged. I loved Greta and Cliff too much to hold a grudge, but I have to admit that I was pretty angry with him. Why couldn't he see things our way? Did law school make him so rigid he couldn't see the other side? The downpour that greeted us as we left the house seemed preordained to fit my mood.

CHAPTER TWENTY-SIX

G reta called me the next morning.

"I'm sorry about last night," she said. "Cliff is really concerned about this case and wants desperately to do the best thing for Mrs. Duncan. Maybe he is taking this one more personally than most, but I've never seen him act like that before."

"I appreciate his passion for the case, but I'm convinced he's got it wrong."

"I don't think you're going to be able to change his mind, Aunt Vi."

"Well, I'm going to keep on doing my own digging to see if I can't find something that would prove to everyone she's innocent."

"More power to you. I hope you're successful." She gave a little laugh. "Even though you know what it would do to Cliff if you proved him wrong."

"Do you think he'd eat crow?"

"Possibly, if you could get her off completely. In fact I'd make sure that he did."

That was worth the effort in itself.

While I swam my laps that morning, I kept thinking about everything we'd learned so far about Ralph's death. One thing was for sure: it somehow had to be an inside job. Someone would need a card to get inside the building. And then they'd need a key to the Duncan apartment. Unless of course Phyllis was so confused she was wrong about the door being locked. If I asked her about it today, I would no longer trust her memory or judgment on it. She'd convinced herself in her despair that nothing was what she originally believed. But at the time we talked right after Ralph's death, she was so sure about it, and she'd had little time then to dwell on her reactions. I felt sure it was true. And apparently the police found no fingerprints on the handle other than hers, Ralph's, and possibly Justine's since she was the only one I knew who visited them. And she was out of town when Ralph was killed. If they'd found any others, they would have questioned them. And, oh yes, the housekeeper.

The housekeeper! They had all been interviewed, but there might be something the housekeeper who cleaned the Duncan's apartment could tell me. That's who I needed to talk to next, and I bet Ty knew who it was since he lived so close to the Duncans. They might even have the same one.

At lunch I asked him who his housekeeper was.

"Linda," he said.

"I don't believe I know her."

"I don't think she does your floor. Nice young woman. Why do you want to know?"

"Does she also clean the Duncan's?"

"Yes. Same day as mine. In fact she did mine this morning, and she does theirs in the afternoon."

"Even if no one is there now?"

"She might not. I believe they have to get the resident's permission to clean if they're gone. With Phyllis in the hospital I'm not sure."

"But she'll probably be on your floor today."

"What's this all about, Vi?"

"I know the housekeepers were interviewed by the police, but, Ty, this has got to be an inside job of some sort since Phyllis was so sure her door was locked. Whoever did it had to have a master key. And they had to be able to get into the building in the first place. Either they had a pass card or someone let them in."

"You think her memory was that good about the door being locked?"

"She told me Ralph always doubled checked it after she went to bed. I don't think he trusted a thing she ever did. And apparently he was somewhat paranoid about safety."

"If she'd only told them she didn't remember or she'd forgotten to do it, she probably wouldn't be in the bind she's in."

"She's naïve, Ty. I don't think it ever occurred to her she was digging her own grave."

Ty shook his head. "What a grand mess."

After lunch he left to run errands and I went to his floor to interview Linda. The housekeepers have big carts that carry all their equipment from mops and brooms and cleaning materials to vacuum cleaner. The cart was parked outside Ginger Willard's apartment. Luckily it wasn't far from the elevator where two chairs and a table provide a place for residents to stop and rest. I could sit there and watch for Linda to come out. Since they spent about an hour in each apartment it could be a long wait. Some kind soul had left a couple of magazines on the table, so I read about "the latest developments in cosmetic surgery." I wondered if anyone at GH was actually interested in doing something like that. Although it was obvious a handful had already gone there, it seemed to me a little late to be contemplating a face lift when most of the residents were in their eighties. Mine had already fallen too far to be remedied. Not that I'd ever considered it. "Take me as I am" is my motto for better or worse.

About twenty-five minutes later Linda emerged from Ginger's apartment with her vacuum cleaner. That was always the last thing they did, so I assumed she was done.

"Linda?" I called as I hurried toward her. She was a young woman in her twenties with dark hair and eyes.

"Yes?" She looked at me blankly because we had never met.

"I'm Viola Weatherspoon from the West Wing," I said catching up to her. "Have you got just a minute? I have a couple of questions."

She looked at her watch. "Yeah. I could take a break of ten minutes or so."

I pointed to the chairs where I'd been sitting. "Can we go sit there?"

"Okay." She began pushing her cart down the hall.

Once we were both seated, I said in a low voice because I didn't want others to hear, "I'm curious about your pass key. It lets you into all the apartments, doesn't it?"

She frowned. "Why do you ask?"

I realized it could sound as if I was about to accuse her of something. No wonder she was frowning.

I leaned over and touched her arm to reassure her. "Don't be upset. I'm not trying to get you in trouble at all. I've been trying to help Mrs. Duncan. I'm sure you know she's been accused of killing her husband."

She shook her head. "She is such a nice lady. I feel so sorry for her."

"I don't think she did it, Linda. I'm trying to find out who did."

Her eyes went wide and her hand flew to her chest. "Not me! I was out sick that day. In fact the day before too. Ask the police. They checked it out."

I hadn't realized that, but if the police had checked it out it must be true. "I'm just trying to figure out how someone could get hold of a pass key. Do you mind telling me where you keep yours?"

She blinked and scowled and seemed to think about it. Finally she said, "I used to keep it on a chain around my neck. But the chain broke, and now I keep it in a pocket in the lining of my cart. She stood up and pointed to a zippered pocket near the top of the frame of the cart.

"Could someone take it out of there while the cart is sitting out in the hall?" I asked.

She grimaced. "I suppose it's possible. But it's never happened. If I found it gone, I would report it right away. I don't think anyone knows it's there." She looked at me seriously. "Except you now, of course."

"I won't tell a soul, Linda. You can trust me."

"I certainly hope so." She looked skeptical.

I prayed she didn't think I was trying to bamboozle her. Had I been in her shoes, I'm not sure how I'd feel.

"What about the other housekeepers? Do you know where they keep theirs?"

"I think most of them wear them on chains like I used to."

That seemed to eliminate the possibility someone could steal their keys. I'd run out of questions to ask her. "Thanks so much. I appreciate your help," I said.

She looked at her watch. "Gotta get back to work."

I went back to my apartment with mixed emotions. I knew now it was possible for someone to steal a pass key, but it seemed that no one had. That didn't help my case any.

Where did I go from here?

CHAPTER TWENTY-SEVEN

A t dinner that evening I told Ty about my interview with Linda.
"So a pass key was available for the taking only as far as we can tell, nobody took it."

"That's about the size of it," I said.

Ty wiped his mouth with his napkin and laid it on the table. He'd just finished his pork tenderloin and spinach, and I was still working on my chicken pot pie which was loaded with gravy and topped with a heavenly thick crust. "You know what, Vi? I'm getting pretty tired of this whole thing. What do you say we take another break? I feel like it's taking over our lives. Do you realize that's about all we've thought about or talked about for the past three weeks or more?"

"I don't think the DA is taking a rest. We have to stay on top of it."

"It probably won't go to trial for months yet. Maybe if we think about something else for a change something new will show up or we'll get a fresh idea. Frankly, right now I'm all out of fresh ideas."

I wasn't a bit happy with his suggestion, but he did have a point. We seemed to be going in circles getting nowhere fast.

"Okay. I'll go along with that. But if I get any brilliant ideas in the meantime, I'm back on the case." I'd had very few brilliant ideas to this point, so I don't know why I thought that was a possibility. But then I thought of Lester. I was pretty proud of my sleuthing on that. Now if I could only come up with other leads that were as fruitful.

I said goodbye to Ty outside the dining room and started back to my apartment. I'd decided to veg out watching some mindless TV show. But by the time I got to the elevator, I thought of Justine. It had been a couple of days since we'd seen her, and I wondered how her nephew was doing. Much as I didn't want to visit with her, I'd had about all the discouraging news I could take, I decided it was the right thing to do.

So I turned around and went back toward the East wing.

I knocked on Justine's door. When she opened it I could tell she had been crying. Her eyes were red, her face flushed, and she had a hankie balled up in her hand.

"Justine! What's the matter? Is it Ed?"

She nodded her head, and a tear slipped out of her eye. "Come in," she said.

We went into the living room and sat down on her sofa together. "Tell me," I said.

"He's on life support, Vi. He's in a vegetative state and he's not going to get any better." She lapsed into a full blown crying session.

Could things get any worse? I put my arm around her shoulders. "I'm so sorry, Justine."

She wiped her eyes and blew her nose before speaking in a trembling voice. "The terrible thing is I have to make the decision whether or not to pull the plug. It's tearing me apart."

What a ghastly situation to be in. I can't imagine being in that position. And yet people have to do it all the time. It's one thing when the patient is old and at the end of his or her life. But when it's a young man, so recently full of energy and spirit, it's quite a different matter. I wouldn't have wanted to be in her shoes for anything.

"Is there some sort of deadline?"

"No. It's just a matter of making up my mind. But every day the bills pile up. Thousands of dollars worth. I don't know who's going to pay them. I guess he does have some health insurance at the place where he worked, but I don't know how much they will pay or for how long. Anyway, it seems awful to rack up hundreds of thousands of dollars in bills that won't bring him back."

"I wish I knew what advice to offer, Justine. But I don't know what it would be. Have you talked to Revered Bill? Maybe he could help you."

"No, I'm not religious. To me this is not a religious dilemma. I don't want anyone to tell me I'll go to hell if I decide to shut off his life support."

"He's not that kind of guy. I don't think anyone is going to tell you that. I guess the doctor would be your best advisor then."

"I already asked him. He wouldn't say. He just said it was entirely up to me."

"Did you ask what he'd do if it were his son lying there?"

She looked at me wide eyed. "No, I haven't. I should do that. In fact I'll do it tomorrow."

We sat there quietly for a few more minutes. She was deep in thought. Finally I got up to leave. "I'm so sorry for you, Justine. Please call me if you think of anything at all I can do." It was getting to be a habit saying those words. I didn't know how on earth I could do anything to help her, but we automatically say them all the time hoping the gesture alone will give some comfort.

I went back to my apartment feeling the weight of the world on my shoulders. I just wanted to wave a magic wand and make it all go away. If only.

I knew Ty would want to know so I called him, but he didn't answer. I figured he'd decided to join in a bridge game for the evening. And they always play later than I stay up, so I decided to share the news with him in the morning.

Sweetie crawled into my lap when I sat down to watch TV. I'd been gone so much lately that I think she was feeling neglected. But this evening we gave each other a lot of comfort. She spent the whole evening there which was most unusual. I wondered if she somehow sensed my need for consolation for she has something of a hyper personality. Generally she doesn't stay in one place for long. But I welcomed her company which always raises my spirits. When she cuddled up against me in bed that night, it was just what I needed to help me go to sleep.

The next morning we had exercise class. Ty had news for me when we met in the café before class.

"Ginger got a new bird. This one is smaller than Lester, a parakeet. A budgie. She decided that since it has a life span of only five to eight years, she hopes to outlive it and not have to worry about what would happen to him if she died first."

"I hope she teaches it clean language so we don't have to listen to the likes of the scatological stuff that came out of Lester's beak," I said.

Ty grinned and shrugged. "Who knows? She might teach it the same words so it will remind her not only of her husband but of Lester too."

I rolled my eyes. "That'll limit my visits with her. I'm glad Greta has said she'll adopt Sweetie when I die. It is a relief to know someone wants her."

"I would have taken her."

"How do you know you're going to outlive me?"

"Because my parents both lived into their late nineties. I have excellent genes." Ty said it rather smugly I thought.

"Well, I'm aiming for one hundred," I replied, turning up my nose. Of course I don't want to make that goal unless I'm in pretty good shape mentally and physically. Not much fun to outlive everyone if your mind and body are shot.

"By the way, that reminds me of something really sad," I said. "I went to see Justine last night. She has a terrible decision to make. Ed's in a vegetative state, and Justine has to decide whether or not to turn off the life support. She's all torn up over it."

"Oh, god. How terrible. Does she have a deadline?"

"No. But imagine having that hanging over your head."

Ty drank his coffee with a thoughtful look on his face. "I'm wondering something."

"What?"

"Do you suppose there's any chance Ed had said he wanted to donate his organs?"

I don't know why that hadn't occurred to me. I'd obsessed some over Perry's predicament, especially when I learned we had the same blood type. But the past few days I'd forgotten about him in all the confusion that had happened since with Phyllis's suicide attempt and Ed's accident.

"Maybe Justine would know. We ought to talk to her about it."

We agreed to call on her after exercise class.

When class was over, I told Ty I needed to go home and shower and change clothes before I called on anyone. He agreed he, too, wasn't in good shape to make a social visit. So we planned to meet in the lobby in half an hour.

Spunky was on her way back to her office, and she and I walked toward the lobby together.

"Did you hear about Justine's nephew?" she asked me.

"Believe it or not we were there when his motorcycle crashed," I said. "He'd known Ralph Duncan so we went to talk to him, but the accident happened before we got a chance to meet him."

"For heaven's sake, what a coincidence. How did he know Ralph?"

"They worked together. Not too happily I might add."

"Did you know he was on life support and not expected to recover?"

"Yes, I talked with Justine last night. She was in a terrible quandary over whether or not to turn it off."

"Well, I heard she's decided to go through with it. In fact, she's on her way to the hospital now to tell them."

I was in shock. I put my hand on Spunky's arm to stop her. "Oh my lord, do you know when she left?" I had to get the word to Ty right away.

"Someone said she was going to leave around ten-thirty." She looked at her watch. "That was about thirty minutes ago."

"I gotta run. I'll explain it to you later," I said as I took off toward the East wing.

I got on the elevator and prayed I'd make it to Ty's apartment before he got in the shower. I rang the bell and pounded on the door when I got there.

After a minute he opened it. "Vi. What on earth?"

"We've got to go," I said, still panting from rushing up the hall. "Justine's on her way to Chapel Hill to tell them to turn off Ed's life support. We've got to get there before they do it and tell them about Perry."

"We don't even know if he planned to donate his organs. Or if they'd be a match."

"We have to take the chance. Don't you want this for Perry?"

"Sure I do. I don't know if we can get there in time though."

"Let's go. *Right now.*" I waved him out the door.

"I'm sweaty and smelly."

"I don't care, Ty. We'll ride with the top down so I can't smell you. And you can't smell me. Okay?" I was getting provoked. We had no time to waste.

"Let me get my wallet and keys," he said as he turned away. He went to the living room and came right back. "Are you ready?"

"I am," I said as I pushed my sweaty hair away from my face. "I don't have a purse or anything, but I guess I don't need it."

We half ran, about all we can do at our age, out to the car. Ty got my ball cap out of the trunk along with his and we took off. It was an overcast day which kept the temperature reasonable, but my feeling of urgency kept me from enjoying the ride. Ty drove faster than usual but was careful not to exceed the speed limit so much that we would get stopped by the Highway Patrol. We finally turned into the parking lot of the UNC hospital about an hour later.

Pulling myself out of the car by hanging on to the door, I yanked off my hat and threw it on the seat. "Let's go, Ty," I yelled. "And let's pray we're here in time."

CHAPTER TWENTY-EIGHT

We trotted at our top speed to the hospital lobby and straight to the reception desk.

"I'm looking for Ed Stillman," I said.

The receptionist looked him up on the computer. "He's in ICU. Are you family?"

"No. Actually we're looking for his aunt who's supposed to be here. It's very important."

"Okay then." She told us how to find the Intensive Care Unit.

Hospitals are the most confounding places to get around I know of. When they expand they grow like Topsy, and it leads to utter confusion for visitors. After a couple of wrong turns we finally found the ICU. Justine was nowhere in sight.

I went to the nurses' station and told them I was looking for Ed Stillman's aunt. "It's vitally important I talk to her as soon as possible."

"She's in a conference with doctors right now," the nurse said.

"We'd like to see her as soon as she gets out," Ty said.

"Why don't you make yourselves comfortable in the waiting room and I'll tell her you're here. What are your names?"

We told her, and she pointed us toward the room. After all our rushing to get here, we were going to have to cool our heels. I just hoped it wasn't too late to intervene.

It was bad enough sitting in a hospital waiting room when a friend or loved one was undergoing surgery, but having to sit there wondering if Ed's life was being brought to an end was excruciating. Neither of us could read a magazine we were so on edge. Ty stood by the window and looked out over the town, while I alternately paced and sat, paced and sat.

About forty minutes later Justine came into the room. "I was told you two were here. How wonderful of you to come to be with me." She came over and took my hands in hers. She looked drained.

"Justine," I said, squeezing her hands. "We're here to help you in any way we can, but also for something else. We understand you're going to turn off the life support."

"Yes," she said, closing her eyes in anguish. "I didn't sleep at all last night. But I decided it was the thing to do."

Ty stood beside us now. "Can you postpone it briefly?"

"Why? Now that I've made the decision, I just want to get it over with."

"Here's the thing, Justine. I have a cousin who's in desperate need of a kidney. He'll die soon if he doesn't get it. Do you know if Ed planned to be a donor?"

She let go of my hands and spread her arms wide in surprise. "I have no idea. We never talked about it."

"It would show on his driver's license," I said. "It will have a little red heart on the front of it if he agreed to donate his organs."

Justine shook her head. "I've no idea where his driver's license is. It might have been with him when they brought him to the hospital, but I've not seen it. I guess I could check."

"Look," Ty said, "the important thing right now is to put this on hold. Can you do that till we get this straightened out? At least find out first if he might be a donor and second to see if there's a match. It could be a matter of life and death for Perry."

"Well, sure," Justine said. "Let me catch the doctors before they get to him. I told them I couldn't bear to watch, so I hope they haven't done it already."

Surely, I prayed, we didn't come so close only to miss out by a few minutes.

Justine was gone for quite a while. The longer we waited, the more our hearts sank. We both paced around the waiting room, unable to sit still. At the time we were the only occupants so at least we weren't disturbing others.

Finally Justine reappeared.

"I managed to stop it," she said. "It really was in the nick of time too. They say that since his kidneys weren't damaged there might be a possibility they could be used for a transplant. They can check to see if Ed is on a donor list, but as his next-of-kin, I can make the decision. But we need to get your cousin in here for tests to see if they are compatible. Can you reach him?"

"I have the information back at home. We were in such a rush to catch you before anything happened, I didn't have time to look it up. But we'll go back right now and contact him."

"Tell him to come to the hospital and report to Dr. Fred Jennings as soon as possible."

The feeling of relief was enormous. I felt I was walking on air as we wound our way back toward the elevator. "Wow, that was close," I said. "I was so afraid we were too late."

"Don't celebrate just yet," Ty said. "If Perry hasn't been able to find a match yet, I think the chances are very slim that it will be a match this time."

"Well, at least there's a chance. Try to think positive, Ty."

"I'll try. I'll try."

From the sound of his voice I didn't think he had much hope, but I knew at least we tried. And I decided then and there that in the event there was no match, I would come forward as a possible donor. After going through all this I felt ashamed of being such a coward.

He didn't drive quite as fast going home now that there was a little less urgency. We both were quiet most of the way, deep in our own thoughts.

Finally he said, "After all this, I hope I can reach Perry. I've no idea where he is."

"That's the blessing of cell phones. He probably hasn't changed his number. You should be able to reach him anywhere."

"Unless he's in a nursing home where they can't have them."

"Do you think he's deteriorated that fast?"

"He seemed to think he didn't have much time left. Well, let's not think about the worst case scenario. We'll just do the best we can."

When we got back to GH I went to Ty's apartment with him while he hunted for Perry's business card. Finally he found it stuck in the back of an address book that was in his desk drawer.

"I should have transferred the information into the address book, but I didn't get around to it," he said. "It's a wonder I found it because I hadn't planned on contacting him again."

"You don't like him much, do you?"

Ty looked sheepish. "Frankly, no. I don't know what it was, but he just kind of rubbed me the wrong way. I guess I found his neediness off-putting."

"How would you feel if you knew you were dying, but a transplant could save your life?"

He pursed his lips. "I suppose I would have acted the same way. I'm not proud of my reaction to him."

"I didn't like him much either," I confessed. "But I surely don't want to see him die." A little voice was whispering inside me that said what I really wanted was to get off the hook myself. I had wanted my guilty conscience to be assuaged because I'd done nothing myself to help him.

"Me either. So let's get on with it."

Ty called the number on Perry's card. Finally he spoke but I could tell he was leaving a message rather than talking to Perry. "Please call me as soon as possible, Perry. It's urgent." And he gave his own cell phone number. When he hung up, he shrugged. "Not there. Let's hope he checks his messages soon."

We realized that we'd missed lunch and we were both hungry so we stayed in Ty's apartment until the dining room opened at five.

"Better take your phone with you in case he calls back," I said.

"I will," he said. "I hate people who talk on their phones in restaurants and dining rooms, but in this case I guess it's important enough to risk offending people."

"We don't know how long they're willing to keep Ed on life support or whether his organs could fail. So, yes, I think it's vitally important."

Ty looked chastised. "Let's go," he said pocketing the phone.

Halfway through dinner his phone rang. Everyone in the dining room stared at him, many with displeasure on their faces.

Ty ignored them. "Yes?" he answered.

He listened for a minute. "I'm in the dining room, Perry. Let me step outside and talk with you. Hold on."

He excused himself and went out into the lobby. People were still looking at me as though we had broken a taboo. All I could do was shrug my shoulders and mouth "sorry." I thought they were overacting, but smiled to myself when I thought how a room full of young people wouldn't have given it a second thought.

About ten minutes later Ty returned to the table.

"Well?" I asked.

"He was going to call the doctor as soon as we hung up. He was so elated. He said his condition has gotten worse since we last saw him. He thinks he doesn't have much longer to live without a transplant. I'm afraid he'll get his hopes quashed when there isn't a match. But I've done all I can do."

"That's all he can ask for," I said. I wasn't going to tell him about my decision to come forward as a possible donor should Ed not be a match. It seemed too much like grandstanding.

CHAPTER TWENTY-NINE

Thursday morning I went to the pool to swim laps. I swam for over an hour and then sat in the hot tub/spa for ten minutes and tried to relax. I couldn't get Perry off my mind. I'm sure part of it was the guilt I felt that I'd never tried to find out if my compatibility went beyond our blood types. Now that there was a slim possibility Ed could be a donor, I very much wanted it to work out. And if there wasn't a match? That would force me to do the right thing.

A thought suddenly occurred to me. What if they determined Ed *could* be an organ donor? Would there be someone on the waiting list higher than Perry who would get the kidney instead? I hadn't taken that into consideration. I knew that when a live donor is involved, the patient doesn't have to be on a waiting list; the donor can give to the patient of his/her choice. But when it comes from someone who has just died, I wasn't sure how it worked. I knew I would find out soon enough.

At lunch I mentioned my concern to Ty. "Do you know if the relative of a dead donor can say where the organs go? What if Perry isn't next in line for one?" I asked him.

"I hadn't thought about that," Ty admitted. "Oh lord. Wouldn't it be terrible if, after all this, the kidneys had to go to the people at the top of the list? And Perry wasn't there? I'd hate to get his hopes up only to have them dashed again."

"Well, we've done all we can. Now we'll just have to wait and see."

"So let's concentrate on Phyllis's problems since there's nothing more we can do for Perry. I know I suggested a break, but let's be honest, we're addicted. "

"Got any suggestions?" I asked.

He traced a figure eight on the tablecloth while he gave it some thought. Finally he said, "Not really. I guess we ought to go visit her and see how she is. Do you think we need to call Cliff and ask him if it's okay?" He asked sardonically.

"I know. I didn't appreciate the chewing out he gave us any more than you did. But he's just trying to do his best for Phyllis."

"Well, so are we. He could at least give us the benefit of the doubt. I suspect his ego is involved. He wouldn't want someone else to solve this case. It would make him look bad."

"No, Ty. I don't agree. I just think he's very worried about her. Cliff has never struck me as an egoist. I'd bet if we did find out who killed Ralph, he'd be thrilled."

He rolled his eyes but said nothing.

We ordered desserts: Boston cream pie for me, fruit compote for Ty. I wished some days they would eliminate the dessert menu completely. I've become a helpless addict of sweets.

When we finished lunch, we went out to his car.

"Let's take a little drive around town first," Ty said as we climbed in and put on our ball caps. "Spring goes by so fast I'd like a chance to admire the early flowers before they're gone."

I agreed it would be a nice respite from all the grief we had been witnessing. The most we'd seen of the redbud and dogwood was on our trips to and from Chapel Hill. Now their bloom was only a memory, but the azaleas were in their full glory. We drove around the neighborhoods with the most beautiful gardens and admired the range of color from white through pale pink, bright red, to fuchsia. Piedmont North Carolina is one of the most glorious places I know in the spring. And when the hot weather comes, crepe myrtle in all its varying shades will carpet the city for the whole summer.

Finally we reached the hospital.

We went to the floor where Phyllis was recovering. But when we got to her room, a stranger was in her bed.

"What on earth?" I asked Ty when we left the room. "Do you think she was released?"

"I didn't see her come home, but then I guess it's possible she could have come when I wasn't around. But how would she get there? Don't you think she would have called us?"

"Since Justine is probably in Chapel Hill at the hospital, I would think so. Let's ask at the desk."

We walked back to the nurses' station and spoke to the one who seemed to be in charge. She was middle aged, buxom, and looked very efficient.

"Can you tell us where Phyllis Duncan is?" I asked.

"Oh, yes, Mrs. Duncan," she said. "She has been taken to the psych floor."

"What?" I was shaken by this news. "On whose orders?"

"I'm sorry," the nurse said. "I can't talk about specific patients. That's all I can say."

"Can we visit her there?" Ty asked.

"Are you family?"

"No, we aren't."

"Sorry, no." She returned her attention to her paperwork to let us know that was that.

"But what if she doesn't have any family?"

She sighed and shrugged. "Rules are rules."

I wanted to argue with her, but Ty seemed to sense my intention and took my arm by the elbow and led me to the elevators. I didn't resist because I knew he had a level head at the moment, and I did not.

After the elevator doors closed, he let off steam. "I can see Cliff's hand in this, damn him. He had her admitted to bolster his claim that she was off her rocker when she killed Ralph."

"You don't know that," I argued. "Maybe her doctor felt she needed the help for her own safety since she already tried to kill herself. As long as she believes she actually did kill Ralph, she's going to be fragile mentally."

"Then we've got to do something about that and as soon as possible."

"Like what? I feel like we've explored every avenue possible. I can't think of anywhere else to go," I said.

"We have to be overlooking something. It's probably right in front of our faces, but we don't see it."

We got off the elevator and returned to the car in a black mood. We had nothing to say to each other all the way back to GH. It felt like Armageddon was hovering over us and threatening to engulf us.

CHAPTER THIRTY

We went by Justine's apartment to see if she was home even though we assumed she was still in Chapel Hill. We thought it was important to tell her the latest about Phyllis. To our surprise she answered the door.

She wordlessly invited us in with a sweep of her arm indicating we should sit on the sofa. She couldn't even muster a welcoming smile.

"Can I get you coffee?" she asked, still standing, though she looked exhausted.

"No thanks, Justine," I said. "We came to tell you we just found out Phyllis is in the psych unit at the hospital." I hated to be so blunt about it but didn't know how to soften the news.

"Oh, lord no!" she cried. "Do you know why?"

"They won't tell us. You know how it is to get information on a patient if you're not family," Ty said.

"Do you think she tried to hurt herself again?"

"I've no idea," I said. I wasn't going to tell her we thought it might have been Cliff's idea to put her there. She would have a fit if she knew.

"I need to go see her then," she said, though she didn't look like she had the strength to go anywhere.

"They won't let you unless you're family," Ty said.

"But she has no one!" Justine was distraught.

"I don't know if you can appeal to the doctors and explain she has no family and you're her closest friend," Ty said. "But you might try."

"Oh god," she said in despair as she sank into a chair, elbows on knees, her face buried in her hands.

We both sat quietly without a word. There was not much else to say that could relieve her misery.

"First Ed, now Phyllis. I don't know how much more I can take." She lifted her head, and tears were streaming down her face.

"I'm so sorry," I said. "This is really a rough time for you."

She nodded as she wiped her eyes with a tissue.

Finally she seemed to gather herself together. "The doctor said before I left UNC hospital that your cousin had contacted him and was coming in for tests today."

"Do you know if Ed's kidney can go to Perry if there's a match even if he's not at the top of the waiting list?" I asked. Perry's life hung on that one question.

She nodded. "They explained it to me. It's called a directed donation. I was told I can't say it had to go only to a child or someone nonspecific like that, but if I know someone who needs one, I can ask that it go to that person."

"Well, maybe some good will come out of this," Ty said. "Though that hardly makes up for the loss of your nephew," he added.

Justine nodded but said nothing, her face a map of misery.

When we left her apartment Ty and I decided to go for coffee even though I don't like to drink it after noon as it keeps me awake at night. But so much was going on in my head right now I couldn't sleep anyway, so it didn't make much difference.

"Now what?" I asked him after we filled our cups and settled at a table.

"Now what *what?*"

"We've made little or no progress helping Phyllis. Where do we go from here?" How many times had we gotten to the point? Why didn't we have the sense to give up? Were we kidding ourselves that we could make a difference?

Ty made a wry face. "Something tells me we aren't the super sleuths we hoped we could be."

I looked at him in shock. "I hope you don't mean you want to give up!" I didn't dare tell him that I'd been thinking the very same thing. But when he said the words out loud, it got my back up. I didn't want either of us to feel like losers.

He stroked his chin with his thumb. "I guess not."

"You *guess* not! Ty, what's going on with you?"

"I hate to say this, Vi, but maybe Cliff is right. Maybe Phyllis would be better off being in a facility that can help her with her mental problems. I feel sure she was depressed long before Ralph died. He was such a rotten son of a bitch it must have been hell living with him. I'm just worried she might try to kill herself again."

"Listen here, Ty-RONE! I agree she must have been in bad shape when Ralph was alive. Who wouldn't under such circumstances? But now she's depressed because she's so sure she killed him. If we can prove to her she didn't, I think she would be a completely different person. She would have something to look forward to for the first time since she married the sorry bastard. I think she deserves to have a little happiness. After all she hasn't got too many years left. I want to make them as good as possible."

Ty leaned back in his chair and gave me the once-over with a sly smile on his face.

"You're something else, Viola Weatherspoon. I knew you were a fighter, but I didn't realize just how stubborn you are. Okay, I'll go along if you've got any idea of what to do next. It's not like my days are filled up with important business appointments or executive decisions."

Now that he had acquiesced, I felt kind of embarrassed because I had no plan. For all my lofty pronouncements I didn't know where to go next. I had to think fast so I didn't look like a total fool.

"Um… remember Farley Lathrop?"

"The drunk in the bar."

"Yeah. He was so plastered when we talked to him I'm not sure we got any reliable information out of him. Remember his boss George Grant at the auto sales told us he and Ralph got into a fight and Farley was hurt pretty bad. Plus, Ralph's neighbor heard Farley threaten him. There's also the fact that Farley said Ralph cheated on Phyllis, but we didn't find out who the woman or women were. Maybe one of them had a husband who decided to get even. I'm thinking we should talk to him again. Try to get the straight scoop."

Ty didn't look excited at the suggestion. Instead he shrugged. "I guess it's something we could look into since we don't seem to have anywhere else to turn. Do you want to go today?" He asked that in a tone that suggested he thought it was a bad idea.

"Why not?"

He looked at his watch. "It's already after three. Kind of a late start don't you think?"

"Oh, come on, Ty. It only takes about forty-five minutes to get to Burlington. Are you afraid of missing dinner or something?"

"No. I just hate to go on a wild goose chase."

"We know where he hangs out."

"Yeah. And if he's at the bar he'll be drunk again and not able to give us any reliable information same as before."

I was getting pretty annoyed with him by this point. "Okay, Ty. I have my own car, and I'll drive myself over. You don't have to go along."

He bit his lower lip. "So you're gonna use blackmail, huh? Like I'd let you go near that bar alone or his home for that matter. Come on, let's get going."

CHAPTER THIRTY-ONE

I wasn't proud of myself for putting Ty on the spot like that. I was feeling as frustrated and discouraged as he was. But I couldn't give up at this point. My mother always told me stubbornness was my middle name.

We didn't have much to say to each other on our way to Burlington. I knew he was peeved at me, and I decided I was better off keeping my mouth shut for a while. No sense in making matters worse. Ty didn't stay mad for long, and I knew his anger would soon blow over. Or at least I hoped so. I had never put it to the test like I had today.

When we got to the outskirts of town, he finally spoke. "Let me do the talking when we get to the bar. If he's there, we'll try to get him to go get a meal with us. Maybe some coffee would sober him up a little."

"You think he'd want to eat at four-thirty in the afternoon?"

"If he's as broke as he seems to be, I think he'd be happy to eat a steak dinner no matter what time of day it was."

The bar had a few more bikes outside it this time. I hoped we could find Farley and leave there as soon as possible. The place gave me the creeps.

When we entered, we saw the same elderly couple sitting at the same table puffing away at their cigarettes with a row of beer bottles between them. They wore the same dingy clothes as before. I wondered if they ever went home. But there was no sign of Farley.

We walked up to the bar. There were even more bikers sitting at it than last time, and they all looked around and stared at us. I stared right back.

"What can I get ya?" The bartender was the same one who had been here before. A large, brutish-looking man with tattoos on his chest that were revealed by the open neck of the polo shirt he wore with others circumventing his arms, I assumed he had twin roles: barkeep and bouncer. He certainly looked tough enough.

"We're looking for Farley Lathrop," Ty said. "Do you know where we could find him?"

The man squinted at us. "You the guys who were in here like a couple of weeks ago talkin' to him, aren't ya?"

"Yeah," Ty answered. "Why?"

"I ain't seen him since. Don't know where he is."

Ty looked at me and I looked at him. Did we scare Farley off? If so, that seemed very suspicious.

"Do you have any idea where he lives or works?" Ty asked.

"He was working the night shift at that chicken place up there on Brant Street. Don't know if he's still there or not."

"Do you know when his shift started?"

"Eight, I think."

"How about where he lives? I understand it was nearby."

"Dunno. He never said."

"Well, thanks, man. I appreciate the help."

Ty turned to me and pointed toward the door. I didn't waste a minute getting out of there.

Back in the car Ty asked, "Want to wait around until eight and see if we can find him?"

"You were the one who thought it was too late to come here in the first place."

"Okay, you were right. We must have said something to make Farley not come back to the bar. Maybe he changed bars so we couldn't find him. Or maybe he left town altogether."

"What do you think our chances are of finding him at the restaurant?" I asked.

"Slim to none."

"But you think it's worth waiting to see? What if we went over there and asked for his home address."

"They wouldn't give it to us."

"Okay, I'm game. Especially since I was the one who wanted to talk to him."

"It's really early, but there's a diner in town that's kind of fun. Built to look like a genuine old fashioned one. It's on Church Street."

"Sure. But since it's so early let's go to the Burlington Outlet Center first. See if there are any bargains."

The outlet center was one of the first in the country to incorporate a whole shopping center for manufacturers' bargain stores. In its heyday, busloads of people came in from all over, including out of state, to shop there. But times had changed, a new outlet center had opened not far down the interstate, and many of the stores had closed. It had the sad air of a dying concern. But there were still great discounts in the last remaining stores, and I always loved an opportunity to shop for bargains.

After I purchased a couple of tops and a pair of shoes, Ty didn't find anything he wanted, we went to the Blue Ribbon diner and had hamburgers, fries, and slaw. Kind of a fun departure from GH's more nutritious meals. He even joined me in ordering a hot fudge sundae for dessert.

We still had a little time to kill so we drove to the park and walked over to admire the restored carousel.

"I used to love to ride on one of these when I was a kid," Ty said.

"Me too. Wish we could ride this one. But it must not open until Memorial Day."

"Let's plan to come back."

"It's a deal."

It was almost eight, so we headed for the carry-out chicken place where Farley worked. It was fairly crowded, but there was no sign of him.

We stood in the order line because we didn't want to cut in front of others even though we only wanted to talk to the manager. When we got up to the register, we asked for him.

"You're lookin' at him."

"We're looking for Farley Lathrop," I said. "We understand he works here."

"He did. But about ten days ago he asked for his paycheck at the end of his shift, walked out the door, and I haven't seen him since. Don't know where he went."

"Can you tell us where he lives?" Ty asked.

"Sorry," he said. "It's against company policy. Wish I could help."

We thanked him and went back out to the car.

"So we scared him off," Ty said. "He's gone to ground."

That sounded suspiciously like CIA lingo to me.

"So do you think he's guilty?" I asked.

"Could well be. Or maybe he was just scared we *thought* he was guilty, and he doesn't have an alibi."

"How are we going to find out?" I asked.

"Maybe it's time to dump all this information in Cliff's lap and let him and his PIs track him down. They have access to ways to find him that we don't."

"Do you think Cliff is going to listen to us? He's made up his mind already, and nothing we say is going to change that. He'll just ream us out again for getting involved."

Ty thought about that for a while. "You know what? I think we have no choice. It would be irresponsible for us not to pass this along to Cliff. Then it's up to him to decide what to do with it. The monkey is on his back."

"I suppose you're right," I said. I hated the thought of going to Cliff again. I loved Greta, and I didn't want Cliff's dismissal of our efforts to come between us. But I decided that Phyllis's future was far more important than my ego or even my relationship with my niece.

"I'll invite them to dinner tomorrow. I don't want to bring it up while we're in the dining room. That could be awkward. So we'll have an after dinner drink in my apartment. Then I can tell him about Farley's disappearance."

"I hope the neighbors can't hear through the walls when he explodes."

"I think he'll have sense enough to keep his voice down. We'll just have to convince him it's a lead worth following."

"Good luck on that."

It was after nine when we got back to GH. We parted ways, and each went to our own wing. Sweetie greeted me with cries of hunger when I opened the door. She's so used to eating at five on the dot, that any time I'm late she acts as though she's been starving for a week. I think she was born with an alarm clock in her stomach.

I fixed her food then decided it wasn't too late to call Greta.

"I'm sorry Cliff was so short with you last Monday. It really isn't like him to be that way," Greta said after we exchanged greetings. "He's really taking this case to heart."

"Well, so are we. That's why I'd like to have you come for dinner."

"You don't have to apologize to him, Vi." *I* had nothing to apologize about I thought. If anyone needed to it was Cliff. But it wouldn't help matters to say so.

"I know that. I just hoped we could come to some sort of a détente over it." I shouldn't have given the impression that I only wanted to make up to Cliff because that was far from the truth. But I hoped we could convince him that this lead was worth following. This was going to take diplomatic skills I'm not sure either of us possessed. Nevertheless, I couldn't live with myself if I didn't try to convince Cliff to follow it up.

CHAPTER THIRTY-TWO

We felt helpless to do anything else until we talked to Cliff. So on Friday we went to exercise together, then Ty went to play bridge, and I went home to read a book. I wanted some time also to get my thoughts together before Cliff and Greta came. I had to be at my most diplomatic self, though lately I'm not as successful at that as I'd like. I sometimes lose my cool and become irritated instead of speaking with enough perceptiveness and tact I can win over my opponent. Actually I did acquire some conciliatory skills as Executive Director of a Girl Scout Council, but somehow in my old age I've lost the will to kowtow.

In the late afternoon I joined the Mah Jongg group. I hadn't been able to play in a couple of weeks, and I was just beginning to get the hang of it. Getting together socially with some of the other residents was a great way to chill out. I knew I should do it more often, and promised myself I would do so as soon as this damn case was resolved.

Greta and Cliff came around six, and we had a very pleasant dinner in the dining room. Everyone pretended that our last get together hadn't ended in rancor. Ty was on his best behavior, and I was trying very hard. Of course it helped that no mention was made of Phyllis. But it couldn't last forever.

"Come up to my apartment for some brandy," I said as we polished off dessert.

"I have to drive home," Cliff said with a bit of petulance in his voice. "The last thing I need is to get stopped and have some liquor in my system."

"Then I'll make a pot of coffee," I said trying to be agreeable.

"It'll keep me awake," he huffed.

"Oh, for heaven's sake, Cliff, quit being such a bore. You can have a glass of water or juice," Greta said as if she were scolding a kid.

"Oh, all right," he said rather grumpily.

Well, this was not going well. Throughout the meal I had thought everything was going smoothly, and I could broach the subject of Farley without Cliff reacting as he had when I didn't inform him about Phyllis being in the hospital. Now I wasn't sure of that at all. This was going to be tricky.

Greta and I walked in front down the halls to my apartment, and Ty and Cliff followed us.

She spoke softly so Cliff couldn't hear. "Sorry about Grumpy. He's had a lot on his plate at work, and I think he's just stressed out right now."

"Well, I better warn you then that I'm planning to suggest something to him that might set him off again," I whispered back.

"About Phyllis's case I assume."

"Of course. I'm as consumed with it as he is. We just don't happen to see eye to eye."

She looked at me with sympathy. "I think it's wonderful you're so concerned about your friend."

"She's not really my friend," I said. "Actually I barely know her. I just don't want her railroaded for something she didn't do."

Greta frowned. "Cliff's not trying to railroad her. He's working hard to do his very best for her."

"I'm sorry. I didn't choose my words very carefully. I know he thinks what he's doing is right. I just don't happen to agree with him."

At this point we reached my apartment door.

Greta greeted Sweetie with a few pats as we entered the apartment, and we all congregated in my small living room. As soon as Cliff settled on the sofa, Sweetie immediately jumped on his lap. *Oh, please,* I thought, *don't do that.* I knew he wasn't particularly fond of cats, and this would only make him more peevish. Greta reached over and picked Sweetie up and cuddled her, cooing her name. I knew she was trying to help me out by eliminating any irritations. I could have hugged her.

"So what can I get you Cliff? Water, Cola, juice?" I asked.

"Water would be fine."

I poured brandy for the rest of us and put the glasses on a tray along with Cliff's water. Carrying it into the living room, I set it on the hassock that served as a coffee table.

I let the conversation drift into small talk for a while before I built up the courage to bring up the subject of Farley. Finally I decided it was now or never.

"Cliff," I addressed him, "I know that you've already decided on your defense for Phyllis. But I couldn't live with myself if I didn't share this with you. It could have some bearing on the case." I looked at Ty for support and continued. "There's man named Farley Lathrop who worked with Ralph Duncan at George Grant's foreign auto place in Chapel Hill. According to George, the two of them got into a fist fight at work and Farley was hurt pretty bad. Later a neighbor of the Duncan's said she saw a man threatening Ralph at his home, and she heard the name Farley. So it seems there was a lot of bad blood between them."

Cliff's face had turned dark, and his mouth was fixed in a hard straight line, but he hadn't said anything. I stopped for a minute unsure of what to say next.

Ty then took up the story. "We tracked him down at a bar in Burlington and talked to him, but he was so drunk we couldn't get much out of him. And God knows if there was any truth to what he said anyway. We left when he passed out."

"We thought we should talk to him again," I said. "But when we went back to Burlington, we couldn't find him. He wasn't in the bar, and he'd quit work right after we'd talked to him. He seems to have disappeared. We think that seems suspicious."

Finally Cliff spoke. "What the hell are you two doing hanging out in bars and talking to strangers who could be psychos? Have you lost your minds?" It seemed he couldn't decide whether he was angry at us for messing with his case again or scared for us because we exposed ourselves to danger. Either way, it seemed we were on his shit list once more. Not that I expected anything different.

"This guy verbally threatened to get Ralph," Ty said. "It seems to us that it would be a travesty if this lead wasn't followed up. We've done all we can. He's disappeared, and we don't have the means to track him down. I'm sure you do."

Cliff glared at him and then at me. He was quiet for a minute.

"I'll make a bargain with you two. I'll put my investigators on the trail of this Farley Lathrop if the two of you will promise me you'll stay out of this case from now on. I just know you're going to get yourselves into deep trouble if you continue on with this ridiculous game of sleuth you're playing. Can I count on you doing that?"

I was holding my brandy with my right hand, and I slipped my left hand behind my back and crossed my fingers. "Sure, Cliff."

Ty had a sparkle in his eye when he said, "Me too."

I had run out of leads and ideas, but I wasn't going to sign on the dotted line that I'd never follow another promising lead if it came up. I was sure Ty felt the same way.

Greta rose and said she thought it was time they should go. I thought that was a very good idea before we got into any more heated discussions. They thanked me and left, but Ty stayed behind.

"So what do you think?" he asked.

"I think we got what we wanted. He thinks he got what he wanted as well, but I had my fingers crossed behind my back when I answered him. Maybe that's childish stuff, but I'm not going to let him push me around."

"Good for you. For the record, I tried to cross my toes. Not sure I accomplished it, but I made the attempt. That's good enough for me." Ty was grinning broadly.

I started laughing and I couldn't stop. "Honestly, we're something, aren't we? Maybe we are like a couple of kids playing detective, but I think we've picked up some good leads, even if they haven't panned out. Maybe they will yet."

"Of course they will. I'm confident of it."

I was feeling less confident, but I wasn't going to tell him that. I thought it hinged on what Cliff's investigators could turn up. I had a feeling Farley was our man.

CHAPTER THIRTY-THREE

We had a weekend facing us with no plans.

"Let's go to the movies and eat out," Ty suggested when he called the next morning. "I haven't been to a movie in ages."

So we went to see some crazy spy thriller that made our little caper seem like child's play. Of course it didn't get our minds off mayhem and murder, but it was all so far removed from reality it didn't matter. As two high performance cars chased each other over winding Alpine roads at eighty miles an hour, I leaned over and whispered to Ty, "Now that makes chasing the bad guys look like fun. Why aren't we having a good time like that?" He knew I was kidding of course, and just threw me a "give-me-a-break" look.

We went to a Chinese restaurant afterward. We never have Chinese at GH, and we both were hungry for it.

I went to bed that night thinking it was fun to have such an ordinary day. But perhaps too many ordinary days might get to be a little tedious. Was I becoming addicted to this investigating?

On Sunday I slept late and spent the rest of the morning perusing every inch of the Sunday paper which I hadn't read thoroughly in quite a while. After brunch I decided to catch up on my stack of books from the library, but I found myself unable to concentrate. What on earth was I going to do with myself now that I no longer had leads to follow and rumors to track down? Was I going to have to take up knitting and crocheting? God help me I hoped not. Had I become addicted to chasing after "bad guys"? Why couldn't I be happy chilling out? At seventy-five I had every right to relax and spend my days playing bingo and watching TV, but I knew I'd be bored to death.

Just as I was ready to go downstairs to meet Ty in the café on Monday I got a call from Justine.

"Great news for you," she said. "Ed is a match for Ty's cousin. They're going to operate tomorrow."

"I can't believe it!" I exclaimed. "After all his attempts to find a match, it finally happened. Have you told Ty yet?"

"I thought you'd like to do that. The surgery is scheduled for eight in the morning. You two might want to be there when Perry wakes up."

"Absolutely. I can't thank you enough for making this happen, Justine."

"Well, I wanted some good to come out of this tragic accident."

I hurried down to the café, my spirits so much higher than they'd been in several days. At least something positive was happening for a change.

Ty was already there sipping on his coffee.

"You look like the cat that swallowed the canary. What's up?" he asked.

"You'll never believe it. Ed's a match for Perry. They're going to operate tomorrow."

Ty almost dropped his coffee cup. "I thought it was such a long shot, I'm stunned. That's great news. Poor old Perry. If he hadn't looked me up, this never would have come to pass."

"I know. We were both pretty annoyed by his aggressiveness. But if my life had been on the line, I'm sure I would have been just as obnoxious."

"Not obnoxious, really, but certainly tenacious," Ty said.

"I think we need to be there for him."

"What time's the surgery?"

"Eight."

"I don't see how we can be there before he goes in, but we can see him when he gets out of the recovery room."

"Why don't we go over around noon? We may have to wait a while, I've no idea how long the surgery takes, but we can take reading material along," I said.

"Come to my apartment about 11:30. I'll fix us some toasted cheese sandwiches before we go. It takes too long in the dining room."

"Okay," I said. "I've got some greens in the fridge. I'll put together a salad and bring it along."

After exercise class Ty had errands to run, and I decided to visit Ginger and see how her new bird was doing.

She seemed surprised to see me when I knocked on her door.

"Vi! How are you? Haven't seen you in a while," she said.

"I know. I've been really busy, Ginger. But I heard you got a new bird."

"I did." Her face lit up. "Come in and meet him."

I followed her into her living room where the cage sat in front of the window. The black bow was gone, and the bird sat eyeing me. He was considerably smaller than Lester.

"This is Jester," she said proudly. "Isn't he beautiful?"

Jester opened his beak, and a string of profanity came forth.

Ginger's face reddened. "Sorry," she said. "I know it can be upsetting to others, but it reminds me my late husband. He was really a great guy you know. He just had a rather foul mouth. But after Lester died, it was so quiet in here I thought I'd lose my mind. So I decided to teach Jester the same words. In a strange way they comfort me."

I wondered what kind of pathology a psychiatrist would label this, but if it made her happy, who was I to object?

"I understand," I said, though I didn't understand at all.

I stayed just long enough that it wouldn't seem rude when I left. I wondered how often she entertained company with her foul-mouthed bird taking center stage. Poor sweet, deluded Ginger.

The next morning I swam laps before making the salad to take to Ty's. I knew it would only stir up gossip if anyone saw me going into his apartment carrying a bowl of food, but I didn't care. This was the first time I'd had a meal in Ty's apartment. In fact I 'd only been there a few times altogether.

After lunch we piled into his car and headed out to Chapel Hill.

We arrived at the hospital around one o'clock and asked the receptionist where we could wait for Perry to come out of the recovery room. She directed us to a waiting room apparently hidden somewhere in midst of the long winding corridors. I felt like we needed Mapquest to find it. "I'll notify the nurses' station on his floor to let you know when they bring him back to his room," she said.

We did eventually find it and settled in for a long wait since we had no idea when we could see him. It was about two hours before a nurse notified us that Perry had been brought back to his room in the renal transplant unit.

When we walked in, we found him dozing. I sat in the chair beside his bed while Ty leaned against the window sill waiting for him to wake up. Finally a nurse came in to check his blood pressure.

"I see you have company, Mr. Richards," she said as she picked up his arm and wrapped the cuff around it.

When she said that, he looked over and a huge smile broke out. "Hi, guys. I didn't know you were here. Why didn't you wake me?"

"You looked so peaceful we couldn't bear to," Ty said walking over to hold his left hand with both of his. "So how are you feeling?"

"Pretty damn good considering. It hurts of course, and I still feel half out of it from the anesthesia, but I can deal with any amount of pain if it means I got a new kidney."

"He's doing very well," the nurse volunteered. "He'll be a new man when he gets out of here."

Perry couldn't stop smiling. "Thanks to you guys. Talk about serendipity. The fact you knew the relative who allowed the doctors to transplant his organs is some kind of miracle."

"It was even more of a miracle that you were a match," I said. "I was so afraid you were going to be disappointed again."

"You weren't the only one, believe me. I was certain I was going to be let down once more. I didn't have much time left either. I don't know if you knew that or not. The docs said it was a matter of weeks now."

All I could do was shake my head. Strange how things turn out. If he had died, and I hadn't bothered to check out whether or not I could be a match, I would have been devastated. Thanks to Ed Stillman at least I'd decided to follow through if he wasn't a match, and I wouldn't have that feeling of guilt for the rest of my life.

We chatted for a while though we didn't want to stay too long and wear him out. While we were talking I noticed a copy of *Zen and the Art of Motorcycle Maintenance* on the bedside table and thought it was a strange choice of a book for Perry. I knew it had been published thirty-some years ago and was a story of a man and his son on a cross-country bike trip. But, basically, it was an essay on philosophical thought across the centuries. Perry was not what I would call a deep thinker. Perhaps it was something he'd turned to as he faced his mortality.

"Say, Perry," I said. "I thought you said you usually read murder mysteries. What do you think about this book?" I held it up for him to see.

"Oh that," he said." I don't guess I'll ever read it. Not my kind of book. Justine gave it to me because she thought I should have something of Ed's as a keepsake."

Somehow I couldn't imagine Ed having read it either. Of course, I never got to know the man, but from what I'd heard about him, he didn't seem the type. Perhaps the word "motorcycle" made him think it was simply about a bunch of bikers. Or maybe he thought it was a repair manual. I probably shouldn't have judged a man I didn't know, but I doubted it was something he'd treasured. It was a nice gesture from Justine in any case.

"Look, do you want to put it in the library there at Glendon Hills?" Perry asked. "I'm not the sentimental type, and someone might as well get some good out of it."

"Are you sure?" I asked.

He nodded. He looked tired and his eyes were half closed.

"We need to go," Ty said. "Will you let us know when you get out of the hospital?"

"Yeah," he said in a weak voice. "I'll be in touch. In fact I'll take you out to dinner. Just a small way to say thanks."

He closed his eyes and was already back asleep.

I picked up *Zen* and we left the hospital.

"I feel a little funny about taking this book. Maybe I shouldn't put it in the library. What if Justine saw it there? I'm sure she would be upset."

"Do you think she ever goes in the library? She doesn't strike me as the reading type."

"I guess I could find out in a roundabout way. I can look at the sign-out pages in the library to see if her name is there. If not, I'll donate it."

CHAPTER THIRTY-FOUR

I was tired when we got back home. I think it was more of an emotional exhaustion than physical. We were just in time for supper so we went directly to the dining room, but neither of us had much to say. I had slipped the book Perry gave me into a carry all I'd brought along to hold the reading material I'd taken to the hospital. If Justine came into the dining room while we were there, I didn't want her to see it.

Afterward we each went to our apartments. I planned to read for a short while before falling into bed.

I remembered when *Zen* came out many years ago. I didn't have much time for reading when I worked for the Girl Scouts. I was busy many nights and weekends with work-related activities that precluded doing much else. I always looked forward to retirement when I could read all the books I wanted. I'll admit that particular book was not at the top of the list of novels and nonfiction I was anxious to peruse. But I was curious about it. It had stirred up so much discussion and controversy that I decided I should at least check it out. I tend to read light stuff. Perhaps something more substantial would be good for me I thought. Maybe I would love it.

After I got into my pajamas and robe I picked it up. I began to read and got drawn in. I knew nothing about the author so I decided to check the back of the book for some kind of biographical information. In the back, between the last two pages, I found a piece of paper with two numbers and a word written on it: 423, 7:30 and Tuesday.

I was about to throw it away when the realization hit me. Four-twenty-three was the number of the Duncan's apartment. Of course it could mean something else entirely, but the coincidence was just too strange. Could the killer have accidently transposed the numbers in his mind and gone into Ginger's place which was 432? I always thought Lester was killed because the perp went into the wrong apartment. This could explain it. And Lester and Ralph were killed on a Tuesday.

What about the 7:30? Obviously that indicated time. And that would have been about the time that Ralph's killer was at Glendon Hills. But why a specific time? I'm sure he (because I always thought of the killer as a man) wanted to make sure Ralph was asleep, but why not go in the middle of the night when there was little chance of being caught?

I knew that Ed had a grudge against Ralph since they worked together. But was that enough to lead him to commit murder several years later? It didn't make sense. And he had to have help to get into the building. Since his aunt Justine lived here it was possible she could have helped him. But she was away at a funeral. This was getting more confusing by the minute.

I called Ty and told him what I found. "What do you think?" I asked.

"I think it sounds like a promising lead. Not enough to really prove anything though."

"You know what? I want to confront Justine with this. I think I can scare her enough by threatening to go to the cops with this information that she might talk to me."

"Or not," said Ty. "Do you think that's wise, Vi? Why not just tell Cliff what you found. Let him handle it."

"I want the answers myself. Besides, after that last showdown with him, he would absolutely blow a fuse. I'm afraid it would permanently damage our relationship. I'm not going to him again till everything is tied up with a great big bow."

"Providing you can get all the proof in a box that you can put a bow on. Those scribbles might not mean what you think they mean."

"I'm an optimist, Ty. My gut feeling is that there is a definite a connection here. And I'm still pissed that Cliff wants us to butt out. I want to show him we're not a couple of kids playing games. We're serious."

There was silence for a minute. Finally he said, "Well, have it your way. I don't think Justine is a dangerous character. She probably wouldn't shoot us. But I want to go with you just in case."

I knew he meant it as a joke, but it did give me pause. But only for a minute.

"I'm in my jammies. Give me fifteen minutes and I'll meet you outside of Justine's apartment."

It was 9:15 so I was sure she'd still be up. I dressed hurriedly and went to the business center on the lowest floor of the building with the note. I ran it through the copy machine before taking the original and putting it in my internal message box in the lobby for safe keeping. I wanted to show Justine the note to force her hand, but I didn't want to take any chances with the original. If she could destroy it, there would be no evidence.

Ty was outside her door and pushed the doorbell as he saw me approach. It took so long for her to answer the door I was afraid she was gone or in bed. But finally she opened it. She was wearing a robe.

"It's kind of late for a social call, don't you think?" she said crossly.

"We came with condolences," I said, unwilling to tell her the real reason for our visit until we got inside her apartment. Otherwise she'd never let us in.

"And we wanted to thank you again for saving Perry's life," Ty added, realizing what my strategy was. "We saw him this afternoon, and he's doing well."

"As you can see, I'm ready for bed. It's been a trying day," Justine said.

"We'll only take a minute," I said.

She stood back and gestured us inside. "Oh, all right. But you realize how difficult today was. It meant they pulled the plug on Ed."

This was tough. I knew she had to be mourning her nephew. But, on the other hand, the two of them might have conspired to kill Ralph. And I had to get some answers.

After we sat down on her sofa, I had to get my thoughts together as to how to proceed.

"We realize how hard it has been for you," I said. "But Perry will never forget your kindness. You gave him a whole new lease on life in the most literal sense of the word."

The frown on her face eased. "I'm glad for that."

"That's why it's so difficult to bring up this other thing."

She looked confused. "What other thing?"

I pulled the copy of Ed's note out of my pocket. "This," I said and handed it to her.

The look of puzzlement soon changed to wariness. "Where did you get this?"

"It just came into our possession. and we know it came from Ed," Ty said. We'd decided in advance not to tell her we found it in the book. Perhaps we would later. Or it would come out at trial. "Do you doubt it's Ed's handwriting? I think it would be easy to prove." I wasn't so sure considering there was so little there, but I hoped that wouldn't occur to her.

"This is ridiculous," she snorted. "This means absolutely nothing." She crumpled up the slip of paper and pitched it into a nearby wastebasket, no doubt thinking she was destroying the evidence. Her attitude had guilt written all over it as far as I was concerned.

"Four-twenty-three is the Duncan's apartment," I said. "And I believe the killer accidentally transposed the numbers in his mind and went into Ginger's instead which is four-thirty-two. That's why the parrot was killed. So it wouldn't wake Ginger up." Everyone at Glendon Hills knew Ginger's parrot died, but only Ty and I knew Lester had been killed. "And this happened on a Tuesday which is written on that piece of paper."

Justine stood up. "Are you guys for real? Or have you been smoking something that's causing you to hallucinate? My nephew has just died, and now you are making these outrageous allegations. I think you should leave."

I was just fishing around. But her reaction convinced me she really did know what happened. Unhappily, though, I was stymied. I looked at Ty and he looked at me. Neither of us could come up with any further arguments. I had probably botched my chances of solving this by confronting Justine too soon. I should have gathered more evidence in order to nail her. Maybe Cliff was right and I should have stayed out of it.

I stood up reluctantly and turned to Ty. "Let's go," I said. "Perhaps Justine's conscience will get to her eventually and she'll come clean."

She looked at me imperiously. "I have nothing to come clean about. Now, please leave."

We started for the door and passed the open kitchen which had a four-foot-high wall that divided it from the living room and entryway. All apartments have this feature and residents use the shelf that tops the wall to dump mail, notices, whatever they have in their hands when they walk in the door. Justine's was as cluttered as everyone else's, and I noticed a ring of keys that also held a white plastic pass card which allowed her to get in the building by the back doors. But what caught my eye was a dark brown stain the shape of a thumbprint on the card, a stain that could have come from dried blood.

I stopped in my tracks, and Ty, who'd reached the door, looked back at me curiously.

My mind was buzzing as I tried to make all the connections.

Finally I picked up the key ring and turned to confront Justine. "This looks like blood on your card, Justine," I said dangling the keys and card in front of her. "Want to bet it's Ralph's blood? I'll wager we could have it analyzed and it would be a match." I had no idea if it would be possible but it sounded good.

"Damn you!" she screeched and tried to grab the key ring from my hands.

I handed it quickly to Ty who stashed it in his pants pocket. "Forget that, Justine," I said. "You're not getting it back. Now, do you want to talk to us?"

Her face crumpled. "Why should I answer your damn questions?"

"Because my niece's husband is Phyllis's attorney. If I give him the information rather than the police, maybe he can figure out a way they won't come down so hard on you. He's a very good lawyer." *In spite of the way he's dismissed my ideas.* "By the way, I thought you were her best friend. Why are you letting her swing for this?"

Justine put her hands over her face and began sobbing so hard her entire body shook. Ty and I sat there quietly and let her cry.

Finally she put her hands down. Tears continued to stream down her face, and she appeared as though she'd aged ten years in the past ten minutes. "I never meant for this to happen to her. It all went so wrong."

"What did happen?" Ty asked.

"Ed was supposed to put arsenic in the coffee. Ralph always prepared the coffee pot the night before and set it to start the next morning at 7:30. Phyllis never drank coffee, and I didn't think the cops would ever detect it. I thought they'd treat it as a heart attack. But for some unknown reason Ralph was up. He *never* got up that early. Phyllis talked about what a creature of habit he was. He always went to bed at a certain time and got up at a certain time. It usually never varied."

"I'm sure Ed had remembered the apartment number wrong. When he went into Ginger Willard's apartment by mistake it made him late." Ty said.

"He might have slipped into other apartments, too, looking for the right one. That must have delayed him just enough that Ralph got up right after Ed finally found the Duncan's place," I added.

"He never told me that. He just said that when he was in the kitchen, Ralph came in and surprised him. He began to threaten Ed, so he pulled a knife out of the knife rack on the counter and stabbed him. Ralph must have stumbled to the living room before he died."

"And when Phyllis found him bloody on the floor, she picked up the knife to defend herself. By the time she got out in the hall, she was in shock," I said. "What I want to know is where did you get a master key to the apartments?"

Justine grimaced and shook her head in despair. She knew we had her, and it wouldn't do any good to lie to us. "Linda's my housekeeper. I happened to see her when she put her key in that zipper pocket on her cart. So one day when she was busy cleaning my bathroom, I went out in the hall, got the key, and made an impression of it in some clay. I knew a key could be made from that if you know the right people."

"And you know the right people," Ty said roughly.

"I *found* someone. I don't generally run with that type." She sounded insulted. I thought that was laughable. She was every bit as much a criminal as those who lolled in jail cells.

"So, I gotta ask. Were you deliberately trying to frame your so-called best friend?" I demanded.

"No! No!" she cried. "I was trying to *help* her! She'd stayed with that bastard all that time even though her life was miserable. She didn't have the guts to leave him. So I decided to get rid of him for her. I planned for it to look like a heart attack. Then she'd be free of him and could participate in the good life here. I never intended for it to turn out the way it did."

"But when the police accused her, you kept quiet. Why was that?"

"My god! That would have meant incriminating my nephew. I promised my sister before she died that I'd look out for him."

"And don't forget—it would have meant incriminating yourself as well," Ty said.

"Yes, well..."

"You decided you'd rather save your own hide than hers," I said. I was so fed up with this woman.

"No, honestly. I thought it would work out. I thought she might have to spend a few months in a mental hospital, and then they'd send her home as cured."

"She could have spent the rest of her life there."

Her face crumpled, and she looked like a child who had been severely chastised. "What was I supposed to do? It didn't turn out right." She broke into more sobs.

"You were supposed to tell the truth and get Phyllis off the hook," I said. "Who needs a friend like you?"

CHAPTER THIRTY-FIVE

We knew we had to do something about Justine that night. If we let it go till morning, she could be long gone. Although we thought we had enough evidence to prove Phyllis wasn't guilty, we didn't want Justine to get away with it by fleeing. And I wasn't going to give her back her pass key which was the most incriminating evidence of all.

I picked up Justine's phone and called Cliff.

"Well, hi, Vi. Isn't it past your bedtime?" he asked. I took it as a snide remark though he probably didn't mean it that way.

"I just wanted you to know I'm sitting across from your perp," I said.

His tone changed dramatically. "What are you talking about?"

"I'm in Justine Abernathy's apartment. She's supposedly Phyllis's best friend. But in fact she and her nephew Ed Stillman plotted to kill Ralph."

There was a moment of silence while he digested all this. "Is this something you can prove?" His voice sounded full of doubt.

"Absolutely."

"And where is this Ed Stillman?"

"Dead."

"*Dead!* What's going on, Vi?"

"It's a long story, Cliff. Ty and I can explain it when you get here."

"You should call the police. They have to take her into custody."

"I promised Justine that you would make it easier for her. Can't you come over now?"

"This is pretty complicated, Vi. Phyllis is my client, remember? It might be a conflict of interest to help Justine."

"Do you want to hear her confession or not?"

"Of course I do."

"Then get over here. We're in apartment 213."

"I can't get in the front door this late. Remember they lock the outside doors at nine?"

"I'll meet you in the lobby then." And I hung up.

Ty stayed with Justine while I went to the lobby to let Cliff in. He was there in twenty minutes with a look on his face that said he hoped he wasn't chasing some fantasy that I'd dreamed up. I could tell he was still in disbelief.

"So what's this all about?" he asked when he came into the lobby. "I love you, Vi, but I hope this isn't a wild goose chase. And what ever happened to the promise you made me a few days ago?"

"My fingers were crossed."

He shook his head and heaved a deep sigh. I was the unruly child who was totally out of control.

I led him over to my internal mailbox, pulled out the note Ed wrote, and handed it to him.

"So what does this mean? A couple of numbers and the word Tuesday."

"Let's go up to Justine's apartment, and I'll explain it to you. But you'd better put that away. She's already thrown away the copy I showed her."

He folded it and put it into his inside jacket pocket. He and Greta must have been out for the evening because he was still wearing a business suit.

He followed me to the apartment, and Ty let us in. Justine was sitting with her head in her hands as if she hadn't moved a muscle since I left.

"Justine, this is Cliff Holcomb," I introduced them. "Cliff, Justine Abernathy."

She barely looked at him before burying her face again.

"So tell me what this is all about," Cliff said, taking a seat in one of the chairs.

"I'll make it as short and sweet as possible," I said. "Justine and Phyllis have been friends for years, and Justine always hated Ralph and tried to talk Phyllis into leaving him. But she didn't seem to have the will to do it. So Justine cooked up a plan to kill him and make it look like a heart attack, thereby freeing Phyllis from his tyranny."

"Didn't you tell me she was at a funeral out of state when it happened?" Cliff asked.

"She was. A perfect alibi," Ty said. "So she convinced her nephew to do it. Probably paid him because he was struggling financially."

Justine looked up and scowled when she heard that. "That's a lie. He did it because he felt an obligation to me. He would never take my money for something like that."

"See what I mean?" I said. "She admits to it."

"So explain the note," Cliff said.

"Ed was late getting there. He'd gone to the apartment across the hall by mistake because he'd transposed the numbers in his mind. The parrot started to squawk so he broke its neck to silence it. He intended to put arsenic in the coffee pot that Ralph had set up the night before to brew at 7:30 in the morning. But, by the time he found the right apartment, Ralph surprised him in the kitchen and threatened him. So he grabbed a knife and stabbed him instead," I explained.

"See? It was self defense," Justine interrupted.

Cliff glared at her. "Not when he was planning to kill Ralph in the first place."

"So how did he get into the apartments?" Cliff asked.

"Justine surreptitiously made a mold of a maid's master key and had it duplicated."

"But that wouldn't have let him in an outside door would it?"

"No, but this would," Ty said pulling the key ring from his pocket and passing it to Cliff. "See that stain on the key card? We're pretty sure it's Ralph's blood."

"Hmmm," Cliff mused as he studied it. "This looks like the final piece of the puzzle."

"We're pretty sure that's Ed's thumbprint," I added.

"You said Ed was dead," Cliff said. "Would you mind explaining that?"

"We knew he'd worked with Ralph, and the two didn't get along since Ralph cheated him out of commissions. When we went over to Chapel Hill to question him we learned he was at a dirt track riding his motorcycle in a race. We intended to catch him there, but while we waited for the race to end, he had a terrible accident, and his neck was broken. He was on life support for a while, but the doctors said he'd never come out of the coma."

"I'd never have given his kidney to your damn cousin if I'd known you were going to do this to me," Justine whined. "You tricked me!"

"We knew nothing about Ed's involvement when we asked you to donate to my cousin Perry," Ty said. "That was a humane gesture on your part, and we'll never forget that. And Perry will be forever grateful."

Cliff shook his head. "My god, this is all so confusing. So the actual murderer is dead."

"I had them turn off his life support just today," Justine said, "right after they took his kidney and the other organs."

Cliff turned to me. "So how did you get this note?"

I couldn't help smiling a bit at the irony. "Justine gave Ed's copy of *Zen and the Art of Motorcycle Maintenance* to Perry as a memento. He in turn gave it to me, and I began to read it this evening. When I became curious about the author, I looked in the back to see if there was any biographical information. And guess what I found there."

Justine's mouth fell open. "What an ingrate! I thought he would treasure that book, and he gave it to *you!?*"

I shrugged. "I guess it wasn't his type of reading. What can I say?"

Cliff shook his head in disbelief. "This has got to be the craziest case I've ever been involved with."

Justine put on her "poor-little-me" face. "Are you going to help me? Vi promised you would."

He gave me a dirty look. "I'll see what I can do for you, Justine. How about you come with me now and I'll take you down to the police station."

"Now?"

"Yes, now."

CHAPTER THIRTY-SIX

Greta called and invited us to dinner on Friday night. We hadn't heard from Cliff since he took Justine to the police station on Tuesday night. We'd learned that Justine was back at GH after posting a very high bail bond. I'm sure they took her passport away from her since she loved to travel so much. She hadn't shown her face in public though. I wondered just how long she was going to lay low. Her arrest had been in the newspaper so the residents at GH knew about it. They often approached me or Ty and asked us what we knew, and we both just shrugged and said "Sorry." We had no intention of telling them about our involvement.

As we got into Ty's car I said, "This should be interesting tonight. After all the times Cliff told us to butt out, I wonder what he's going to say now."

"Do you think he will apologize?" Ty asked.

"I don't know. Do you want to make a bet?"

"Sure. I'll bet you a hot fudge sundae at Cold Stone Creamery that he doesn't."

"I'll take you up on that."

Greta greeted us with a big smile when we rang the doorbell. "So here are our super sleuths," she said.

She hugged me tightly and kissed my cheek. She gave Ty a hug too.

Cliff came into the living room with a tray of drinks just as we entered. "Here we go," he said. "The usual."

"So what happened Tuesday night?" Ty asked as we sat around the coffee table where Greta had laid out crudités and dip. She'd concocted some kind of wonderful spinach and artichoke dip that I couldn't get enough of.

"She had to spend the night in jail. She was arraigned the next morning, and the judge set bail at half a million bucks."

"What did they charge her with?" I asked.

"Accessory to second degree murder. She was lucky it wasn't first degree."

"So how did she afford to pay the bail?"

"Justine has plenty of money. It cost her ten percent or fifty thousand for a bail bond."

"She travels all the time," Ty said, "so I'm not surprised she could afford it."

"She won't be traveling anytime soon," Cliff said.

"So did I mislead her by telling her you might be able to help her out?" I asked.

"Once I get the DA to overturn the charges against Phyllis, I'll do what I can for Justine. I'm not above taking her money," Cliff grinned. "But in her case I can't see that there is much in the way of mitigating circumstances. We should probably hope for a plea bargain, though I feel sure she'll spend some time in prison."

"Poor Justine," I said. "And she thought she was helping her friend."

"You know, she might have convinced you of that, and it probably had something to do with it. But she told me confidentially on her way downtown that Ralph had put the moves on her some time back. She said she barely escaped being raped. I think she hated the SOB and wanted him dead for that."

"I know he had extramarital affairs," Ty said. "But I never heard any allegations of rape or attempted rape. I wouldn't be surprised if he put the moves on her, but I seriously doubt he would have raped her."

"As they say, only the two people involved know for sure. And one of them is dead. There's no way to prove it one way or another," I said.

"I can't use it in her defense without some kind of corroboration. And I don't see how I can get that." Cliff stood up. "What say we go eat dinner?"

"Tell us first about Phyllis," I said. "Will she be coming home now?"

"I went to the hospital yesterday and told her about Justine. She was shocked, of course, to think her best friend had her husband killed. But the realization that she didn't do it herself will, I think, get her out of the psych ward very soon. I spoke to the doctor, and he seemed to think that now he can help her deal with the trauma, and that she should be well on the road to recovery."

What a relief that was. As soon as she got back to GH I intended to see that she got out of her apartment and became involved in some of the activities there. I wanted to make sure all the residents embraced her now as a valued neighbor. Most of them barely knew her.

As always, Greta had put together a wonderful meal. She served veal scaloppini, chunky mashed potatoes and zucchini squash. The conversation during dinner was much more cheerful than it had been the last couple of times we'd had dinner with them. We'd almost finished the meal when Cliff said, "By the way, guys, I think I owe you an apology. I know I gave you a hard time about getting involved in this case. But I'll have to admit you did an amazing job! I was always convinced that Phyllis was guilty."

"And I was just as sure she was innocent," I said. "I simply couldn't see that poor woman spending the rest of her life in a mental hospital. She'd had such a crumby life up to this point I wanted her to enjoy whatever years she had left."

"Well, she certainly owes you two a debt of gratitude. I hope she'll realize that."

"I don't care whether she appreciates us or not. She'll probably think of us as the ones who ruined her best friend's life. But we know we did the right thing. Don't we Ty?"

"We did. And, Vi, if you hadn't dragged me into it, I would have let it go as another tragic incident. You were the one who insisted we get involved."

"You worked every bit as hard as I did."

Greta raised her glass of water. "Here's to our two amazing detectives."

Now I was getting embarrassed. "What say we change the subject? Seen any good movies lately?"

After she cleared off the plates, Greta asked, "How about some apple pie you guys?"

I looked at Ty and grinned. "Thanks but no. Ty here promised to take me for a hot fudge sundae at Cold Stone Creamery."

"And I think we have a date to check out a carousel in Burlington," he said.

"You're right. I'd forgotten about it. How about this weekend?

Proof

Made in the USA
Charleston, SC
23 May 2012